WHEN SHE LEAVES YOU

◆◆◆◆◆◆◆◆◆◆◆◆◆◆◆◆

IAN MACDONALD

MILLENNIUM BOOKS

First published in 1995 by
Millennium Books
an imprint of E.J. Dwyer (Australia) Pty Ltd
Unit 13, Perry Park
33 Maddox Street
Alexandria NSW 2015
Australia
Phone: (02) 550-2355
Fax: (02) 519-3218

Copyright © 1995 Ian Macdonald

This book is copyright. Apart from any fair dealing for the purposes of private study, research, criticism or review, as permitted under the Copyright Act, no part may be reproduced by any process without written permission. Inquiries should be addressed to the publisher.

National Library of Australia
Cataloguing-in-Publication data

Macdonald, Ian.
When she leaves you.

ISBN 1 86429 020 X

1. Divorced men–Life skills guide. 2. Widowers–Life skills guides. 3. Single men–Life skills guides. 4. Separation (Psychology). I. Title.

306.89

Cover design by Bybowra Design Group
Text design by Warren Penny
Typeset in 10.5 pt Stone Serif by Egan-Reid Ltd, Auckland
Printed by Australian Print Group
10 9 8 7 6 5 4 3 2 1
99 98 97 96 95

ACKNOWLEDGMENTS

To Steve Biddulph
Of the many people who have helped me in invaluable ways I must single out two for whom I have special gratitude. The first of these is Steve Biddulph, author of *Manhood*, a book which I commend to all who have sometimes wondered about the role of men in today's society. Steve was generous with his time when I'm sure he had little to spare, and read an early draft of this book. His comments and suggestions were very significant and most have been adopted.

To Bettina Arndt
The second person for whom I have very special thanks is Bettina Arndt who also read the manuscript and carefully annotated her comments which included some very cogent reasons for my re-thinking some sections of the text. Although we had never met I approached Bettina on a "cold canvas" on the basis of her recent writings. I believed that she above anyone writing on the subject of relationships would have invaluable insights and a better balanced attitude than almost anyone I could think of. My hopes were more than justified and her contribution is a major one.

To Pam Walker and Maggie Vickers
Many other people have encouraged and helped me in the writing of this sometimes painful document. I would particularly thank Pam Walker for her careful checking of the manuscript and the addition of some advice about politically incorrect terminology! Maggie Vickers also has my grateful thanks for her calm judgment and wide understanding of this and so many other aspects of relationships.

To the men who shared experiences
Finally and most particularly I thank all those men with whom I shared so many hours of talk, sometimes painful and almost always frank. They must remain anonymous because all the episodes I have referred to probably touch other people at a very personal level. I feel very honored to have had the trust and confidence of these people and hope they share my wish that their experiences may, through these pages, help other men to deal with the trauma of broken relationships.

CONTENTS

Acknowledgments iii
Preface 1

Part One
SURVIVING

Separation	7
Grief	13
Loneliness	17
Anger	23
Violence	27
Blaming	31
Friends	35
Celibacy	39
Survival	43
Housekeeping	47
Diversions	51
Marketing	55
Options	59
Counseling	63
Stereotypes	67

Part Two
GROWING

Beginnings	73
Passion	79
Parenting	83
Stepparenting	87
Caretaking	91
Life-styles	95
Redefinitions	99
Contracts	103
Religions	107
Monogamy	111
Divorce	115
Custody	117
Access	119
The Law	121
Property	125

Malcolm's Story 127
Nathan's Story 131
Silver Linings 135
Bibliography 138

Preface

*'Tis better to have loved and lost
Than never to have loved at all.*
ALFRED LORD TENNYSON

This book is for men who have loved and lost.

It is for the countless men who through death, desertion or divorce find themselves alone and lonely. It is for men who are desperately trying to find the wisdom to survive without a partner and to get their lives back together.

We've all heard time and again the ever-growing divorce statistics but in addition to these, no one can guess at the number of men who will come to the end of de facto relationships, which might well be more important to them than a registered marriage.

This represents enormous suffering and unhappiness and in most cases the men concerned are ill equipped to deal with it. The purpose of this book is to help men understand some of the emotional complexities of separating from a partner and to help them to deal with emotional reactions that they are often experiencing for the first time. For many men the sudden desperation at being alone and the anger and grief they are feeling will be almost unbearable.

To survive we need to learn the skills to put our lives into some order again. Time may be the great healer (as well-intentioned friends keep telling us) but this will remain no more than a platitude unless we learn to take charge of our lives and give time a chance to do its healing.

This is not a heavy psychological treatise, nor is it intended to offer magic remedies for unhappiness. It is simply the result of my personal experience and that of other men who have been frank enough to discuss their own experiences with me.

I hope these pages will provide some hope and guidance to men who may feel they are experiencing something unique. I hope they may get some comfort from the knowledge that there is an army of men out there going through the same kind of distress and that most of them will survive and go on to lead full and happy lives. I would like to believe that most of the men reading this will come to the point as I have after a long and difficult journey, when they can say with truth: "I am the captain of my soul, I am the master of my fate."

When She Leaves You is specifically addressed to men and I make no apologies for this (in fact, much of what I say can apply to women suffering the same kind of distress after a breakup). Women, however, have very sensibly set up their own networks and at both informal and formal levels have access to a lot of support. In addition there is a big body of self-help literature addressed mainly to women. This is not to draw an odious comparison; it is simply that I believe the imbalance needs to be redressed.

It also needs to be said that I am not attempting to comment on causes or fault in the breakdown of relationships. There are books dealing with these matters and I am in any case not qualified to deal with them. I have made the assumption that I am addressing men who have come to the point of accepting that their relationship has irretrievably broken down. My aim is to give hope to men who have perhaps not yet journeyed as far as I have down the road to recovery, and to help them face the future with strength and confidence.

I also discuss some aspects of forming new relationships and suggest some ways of recognizing mistakes of the past to avoid future relationship disasters.

Whatever the cause of a parting, whether through death or a breakdown in the relationship, every man with a grain of sensitivity will experience an intense period of grief. There is no way this can be avoided, and the only comfort is that it does in due course pass. The essential first step is to manage this grieving period, to minimize its destructive effects and indeed turn the experience into a positive emotional force.

PREFACE

Grief can produce powerful energy that can be directed to an intense period of self-discovery. In a letter to me Stephen Biddulph said "this is often the real self-discovery time of a man's life—when he . . . takes a hard look at himself and changes in some major ways." By taking a positive attitude to our grief and acknowledging its force we can get in touch with all kinds of deeper feelings that we may have repressed for years. Eventually we will experience a sense of heightened awareness as we allow our emotions to emerge from the prison in which most of us keep them in restraint.

Some years ago I was working on a one-man exhibition when a sudden split-up threw me into a state of despair. I asked the gallery director to cancel the show, but she wisely declined, suggesting that I channel this grief into my work. I kept working and the show was, as they say, all right on the night. More important perhaps was the psychological effect of the enforced discipline on my ultimate recovery. It provided me with a responsibility to someone else to put my own unhappiness aside and get on with the job.

Part One
SURVIVING

SEPARATION

She went her unremembering way.
She went and left in me
The pang of all the partings gone
And partings yet to be.
　　　　　FRANCIS THOMPSON

The end of a loving relationship can be the most traumatic tragedy in the lives of ordinary people. Whether it is the result of death or a parting, the grief will be acute, even unbearable, for anyone with real feelings for their partner. It is a wound that will heal only with time and treatment. For some people I know it seems to never fully heal even though they are able to live full lives and may have entered a new relationship.

From my reading I learn that the great majority of marriage separations are initiated by women. Very frequently men are totally unaware of the impending disaster. Sometimes they come home to an empty house with furniture and possessions gone. Many of these men say they had no idea that there was anything wrong with the relationship until their partners had actually left them.

These men are stunned by feelings of shock, disbelief, rage and depression. Their emotions can boil over into uncontrollable anger and normally gentle men can become dangerously violent. There is sometimes only a hairsbreadth between self-restraint and physical violence, even murder. The French acknowledge the force of these violent emotions in the term *crime passionnel*. If there is a lover involved the element of jealousy becomes a further catalyst in the explosive situation, like throwing petrol on a smoldering fire. Sometimes men in this state will direct their anger against people outside the issue and relatives, colleagues, workmates, even their children can become the focal point of their rage.

Too often the emotional morass becomes so uncontrollable that the man loses all control and suicide can be seen as the only option. Some men succumb to the impulse; others allow themselves to die from the slow suicide of self-destruction by neglect or drug or alcohol abuse.

Rod is in his thirties and has a daughter aged five. His wife, the little girl's mother, left home when the baby was two to live with another man and Rod has taken care of her ever since. A couple of years ago Rod met a single girl and moved into her house which he helped her to restore. He is a builder and he spent a lot of time and money to make the derelict place into somewhere pleasant and comfortable to live. It was a labor of love and he was happy that he was able to make a real contribution to their joint lifestyle. They had intended in due course to marry and have another child. He was providing all the family income and felt in every way that the relationship was permanent and stable. Meg, the little girl, was secure in the knowledge that she had a loving father and a de facto stepmother who seemed genuinely fond of her.

Returning from a country trip where he had a major project under way, Rod was appalled to learn that another man had been staying in the house in his absence. He was introduced as "my new boyfriend" and Rod was asked to pack his belongings and leave. The only explanation he got was that "no relationship is forever." His first reaction was white-hot rage. "I wanted to beat the crap out of the guy," he said. "I could easily have killed them both there and then if Meg hadn't been there begging to be taken away."

Rod now lives in a small apartment with Meg and spends most of his time with her. He has a couple of women friends but has no permanent relationship and is afraid of forming one. He is a gentle man but he has become cynical and feels he can't trust another woman. He is trying to discover what it is that makes him so vulnerable to emotional hurt. He feels that all the men he knows in apparently sound relationships are those who treat their partners with aggression and even a degree of violence, at least verbally.

SEPARATION

Bart has come to the end of his third marriage to a younger woman with two teen-age children. After twelve years of marriage she announced that she wanted "out." She has given him no explanation of why she wanted to end the marriage other than to say that she is sick of being 50 per cent of a couple and needs to find out who she is. She refused to attend counseling sessions and after several attempts at reconciliation, Bart left the family home. He is understandably bitter that after supporting and fathering her children for all those years he has been rewarded with a callous dismissal. It was only weeks before the split that they had been planning how they would change their life-style when the children left home, which they anticipated would be imminent.

Not all partings of course are so blatantly the result of a unilateral decision. I have friends whose parting of the ways was mutually agreed and who meet periodically for a meal and a chat. In my experience this is unusual because one partner generally expects more than the other is prepared to give in such a casual relationship. In particular, sex is likely to be an issue and many men would feel that it is difficult to adopt a platonic friendship with someone who has been a lover. Sometimes it's possible after a lot of healing has taken place, but when the wounds are fresh I think it is asking something that is either impossible or undesirable.

Some men have expressed to me the feeling of relief that has come from finally parting with a long-term partner. This is understandable when a marriage has become mundane and the excitement has gone out of it. One man I know threw himself into a series of sexual encounters almost straight after leaving home and even joked about "having to put a boy on to cope with the workload." Within a few weeks of this profligate life and the unaccustomed freedom, he realized that there was more in life than casual sex, and he became very lonely.

Whether we part in sorrow or in anger, whether the scene is chaotic or calm, we will have to face a period of great sadness. We need to acknowledge that grief is a real and tangible force that we have to deal with. We must stop the futility of regret from turning our attention to the past. This is a time when it is easy to pretend that nothing is wrong and if we deny reality strongly enough it will all go away. We simply have to remind ourselves brutally that we are finally and irrevocably alone. It's easier to remember the good times in a relationship and the shared happiness than to remember the bad times. But if we are to survive we must constantly remind ourselves of the negative aspects of the relationship that have led to our present dilemma.

When do we finally acknowledge that it is over for good? Both Rod and Bart pleaded with their partners to come with them to counseling. Both women refused and would not entertain any idea of a return to the relationship.

For both of them acceptance came only after they had made almost mendicant appeals to their partners. For others it may be less dramatic and in many cases of course the parting is something which has been discussed and agreed to. I know several cases where trial partings have been arranged, and one where the relationship was resumed after a period of separation. In one case both partners left to go into other relationships but returned together after some months on discovering that the old relationship was better for both than the new ones had proved to be. It seemed to be a happy ending for this couple but one has to consider what the abandoned partners may have suffered.

Sometimes the partners themselves slam the door so firmly that it can never be opened again. We can so easily when in a state of crisis say or do things that can never be recalled. When an old friend of my father told me that he and his wife were separating after nearly fifty years of marriage, I was shocked. They had always seemed to represent the best qualities of a lifetime partnership and always seemed to me as a boy to be a very loving and kind couple. He told me that they had "said unforgivable things to each other which can never be forgotten." Some things in our lives are unforgettable and may be unforgivable too.

Roy was a successful small businessman with what seemed to

me to be an enviable life-style. Comfortably off, he had a very pretty wife and three children and they lived a quite social and it seemed to me, exciting life. One day I learned from a mutual friend that he had shot himself. It seems that his wife had taken a lover and constantly taunted him about his lack of sexual prowess. No one will ever know whether there was a problem in that regard but again she had refused to attend counseling and would not listen to his repeated pleas for a new start. Perhaps he would have been saved from this terminal solution if he had been able to talk to someone about his situation, but he apparently was unable to admit to anyone how unhappy he was and most people had no idea of the turmoil that was racking his mind.

Bart is still mystified as to the cause of the breakdown. "We never had a cross word in twelve years," he says. "I've been a good provider, I don't get drunk, I've been faithful all those years, I almost always remember to take the garbage out, I play with the kids . . . Where did I go wrong? She's had a few lovers since we separated and she still thinks I'm the only one she really turned on to."

Several reconciliation attempts failed and he even took her on a holiday after the parting. "It was a very passionate week," he recalls, "but we were hardly home when she was off again with a guy she had a brief and rather public affair with." To this day he has no idea why this affectionate pleasant woman "jumped ship" as he calls it, and got into some bizarre relationships as soon as she had found her new "freedom."

Of course not all marriages end because of a wife's desertion. It takes two to tango as they say, and outsiders can sometimes see sides to a relationship that the main players may never be aware of. The fact remains that in the majority of breakdowns men are left bewildered and hurt because they simply don't understand what went wrong. Women on the other hand often say that they had been trying for years to tell their man what worried them. It seems that even in this enlightened age communication between the sexes is by no means universal.

If all this sounds depressing and negative, let me say that most of the people I have referred to here have survived and have gone on to find happiness either in their own company or in a new relationship. I have dwelt on the negative aspects of separation because this is the way it is for most of us immediately after a breakup. We have to recognize that we are not alone and that most men do emerge from these disasters stronger and more resolute than ever. The road to recovery is in our own hands.

The first positive step in dealing with the trauma of separation is to acknowledge that it has happened. We have to stop pretending that it is a bad dream that will go away in the morning. Once every reasonable attempt has been made to effect a reconciliation we should recognize that it is not going to change and the pain will only be exacerbated by attempts to mend something which is destroyed beyond repair.

GRIEF

*In every parting there is
an image of death.*
GEORGE ELIOT

Grief is the inevitable and immediate consequence of any parting and it will be much the same whatever the cause of the breakup. Death of a well-loved partner is something so shocking and so final that we tend to think of this as the ultimate grief. I believe that other reasons for the ending of a relationship can produce equally intense and even more distressing forms of grief.

I have personally survived both kinds of grief and my experience was that there was little to choose between them in terms of suffering. One significant difference I experienced was in the strength one gains from the knowledge that death is so final. A broken relationship can have the disturbing aspect of unfinished business. Sometimes indeed it does remain unfinished for a time, and may lead to endless and distressing contact with the estranged partner.

My first marriage ended with the sudden death of my wife from a heart attack. It was a good marriage in every sense. We had four fine children and we had enough money to live reasonably well in a large old elegant house. The pattern of our lives was fairly predictable and we looked forward to the time when our children were older and we could enjoy the mature years in a kind of "golden pond" scenario of peaceful contemplation.

I was forty-one when my orderly world was shattered forever. I spent the next three months in a state of pure shock, as I now realize, although I pretended to be carrying on as normal. I was in fact dysfunctional and my job was only sustained through the efforts of a loyal staff and a lieutenant who took discreet control until I was able to function rationally again. If Hugh should read this I would like him to know that my gratitude for his generous support has never diminished.

Many years later I was to experience another separation. The bonds of a ten-year marriage were broken for reasons I still don't understand. I was shocked to find myself in a state of abject despair and real grief. Anger, sorrow, jealousy and a huge sense of injustice became my witches' cauldron of seething emotions that left me helpless and out of focus. I got closer to understanding the suicide's emotions than I ever have before or since.

Malcolm is a good friend who has recently had a similar parting from his second wife. His grief has been profound and has had a pattern with which I am only too familiar. For him there is an additional pain in that it has opened up old wounds left by the death of his first wife by suicide many years ago. He has come to the realization that he had never completed the grief process after that awful tragedy. Now he is trying to deal with a second disaster and the first is not yet disposed of.

It took me a couple of decades to realize that my own grief had never been dealt with properly. The need to keep working, to care for children and above all to maintain the appearance of stability had swept the act of grieving away to where it would not intrude upon the more immediate problems of survival.

Malcolm and I have paid dearly for not having dealt with our grief when we should have. I would like to think that if I achieve nothing else I may help other men through these pages to come to terms with their grief. If we are to survive and grow, grief has to be addressed and laid to rest along with the flotsam and jetsam of our old relationship.

The first step in learning to deal with grief is to understand what it is. Some therapists will tell you that it has a pattern of predictable progress. I have personally not been able to discover this and my experience has been that there is a complex mixture of emotions which come and go with diminishing intensity as we work through them.

The first and I believe the most easily dealt with of these

emotions is shock. Shock is largely a physical condition caused by a act over which we have little control. We react to shock in a number of recognizable ways and it is sensible, if the symptoms of shock are profound, to get some medical help for them. High blood pressure, palpitations, hyperventilation and panic attacks are familiar aspects of shock and can be dangerous if not controlled.

The more painful feelings I recall are those of depression, anger, guilt, hostility and above all a sense of numb isolation from the world. Our loneliness becomes something palpable and we think we are the only lost soul in the world. Our feelings sit on top of one another like an obscene pyramid, an ugly conglomerate of bad emotions which we can neither define nor dismiss. We feel helpless against this great mountain of grief.

Our natural reaction is to hope that it will go away. We want to ignore it or to find some distraction to ease the pain. Alcohol is a readily available solution and many men seek relief with this palliative. Tragically some of them become addicted permanently and join the ranks of the alcoholic. Fortunately most of us come to the realization that the awful depression of hangovers is only adding to our wretchedness.

Plunging into a new relationship is a natural response too, and some men have multiple affairs in search of the comfort they hope will release them from the burden of grief. Often these men find that happiness eludes them and they end up in unhappy alliances. Sometimes they discover in time that these casual sexual encounters are far from satisfying because they are based on the wrong motivation. One friend tried to solve his problem with prostitutes and ended up by hating himself for having created this extra burden of guilt. It was also costing him a lot of money and as he told me once, "Sometimes I spent good money just to talk to them."

These and other escapist tactics are not only ineffective; they are downright counterproductive. If we are to get on with our lives we have to finish the grief process—the hard way. Until we have disposed of our grief we will never be able to find inner peace. And until that happens we will not be able to form another relationship.

The average Anglo-Saxon male is not well equipped to deal with grief. We have been brought up to believe that expressions of grief are unmanly, embarrassing, unnecessary. I attended my first wife's funeral without shedding a tear, more concerned with failing to greet some friend or relative who might have been offended by my apparent rudeness. By the same token I accepted my mother's judgment that my children should not be exposed to the distress of the funeral. I believe I deprived them of the opportunity to express their own grief as they were entitled to, young as they were.

It was twenty years before I finally let go my pent-up grief while I was working with a therapist friend during a rebirthing session. I had a huge spontaneous unrestrained session of howling, sobbing sadness. If you haven't already acknowledged your grief my advice is to let it all hang out! If you feel like shouting, screaming, sobbing, yelling, raging . . . do it.

Don't be ashamed to admit that you have a big parcel of feelings on board. Weep for your sorrow; rage against the injustice; let your resentment and hostility have full voice. Cry about your guilt and scream over your fears. If you can find someone to help you release all this stuff don't be afraid to let them in. If you're lucky enough to have friends who understand, ask their help. If not, there are professional counselors.

Friends during this period of grief are worth their weight in gold, but be aware that if they haven't traveled the same road as you they may not be able to understand the depth of your grief. Don't ask them to take on board a load they may not be able to identify. Be grateful that they tolerate your moods—it may be all they are capable of doing.

LONELINESS

Oh that 'twere possible
After long grief and pain
To find the arms of my true love
Around me once again.
ALFRED LORD TENNYSON

Next to the grief of parting I think loneliness is the most insidious of the emotions we experience after a breakup. Loneliness can be overwhelming, crippling and unless we learn to control it, it can destroy any chance we may have of recovery.

Loneliness follows you like a shadow wherever you go. Lose yourself in the wilderness and you are beset with the awful feeling that there is not another human being in the world who cares whether you live or die. In a crowded city street you feel alien. Everywhere there seem to be happy couples absorbed in the warmth of their affection. Old people with decades of togetherness bonding them hold hands as they walk about together. Young couples embrace without embarrassment and remind you poignantly of past happiness. It seems in these dark times that only you in the whole world are alone with no one to tell your sorrow to; no one to cry with; no one to hold on to in the watches of the night.

It's at this point that you start to believe that this loneliness is here to stay. A black despair can bring you to the point of madness and you start to see yourself facing a bleak and degrading future as senility takes over your life. You wonder how you will face a bleak future in an old men's home, or even worse that you will someday look like the old derelict in the park with his bottle in a paper bag.

If you are feeling all this, believe it, this is the bottom of the emotional barrel and there's nowhere to go now but up! Stay away from parks where derelicts gather and find somebody positive to talk to. It doesn't matter what you talk about, but the very act of communicating with another human being is a vital lifeline. Try to find friends who have been through a period of loneliness themselves. For people who have led secure sheltered lives it is sometimes impossible to understand just how acute your problem is.

At this stage you will probably be dealing with two big emotional intrusions. The first of these is a severe fear of the future which may cause panic attacks or at best, a feeling of pervasive apprehension about your destiny. And the other emotion is the overwhelming sorrow for the past that is lost. Both are an exercise in futility simply because there is absolutely nothing you can do about either. All that matters, and the only thing that should concern your mind, is the present moment; this is the only thing over which we have control.

The first step in coming to terms with the present moment is to accept that aloneness is not the same thing as loneliness. Indeed loneliness can be most acute when we are with other people. So loneliness is in fact nothing more than a state of mind. We are now dealing with feelings rather than circumstances and feelings are something we can manipulate if we want to. If we accept that we are in charge of our minds then we must acknowledge that we can alter our feelings. And the feeling of loneliness is no different or more permanent than any other.

When loneliness becomes simply unbearable you will need to resist the impulse to try and neutralize the pain by forming a relationship with the first available partner. The lonely hearts columns testify to the fact there are people out there who are desperate for companionship. Some people seem incapable of surviving alone and will grasp the first hand of friendship and cling to it like a drowning person seizes a straw. This compulsion is common to both sexes and I know several people who, faced with loneliness, have jumped into and out of unhappy liaisons with disturbing rapidity in a search for comfort. They will tell you that sex is a factor, but most admit that the desire to have someone to hold on to is the main incentive.

People who succumb to this indiscriminate instinct to couple are very vulnerable to exploitation. They are likely at best to endure an unacceptable relationship for as long as they can, then go through the trauma of separating once again. At worst they may become the victims of outright exploitation and find their personal assets at risk. There are people whose exploitation of lonely people is a calculated activity, and they come in the guise of sympathetic women as well as protective men. While most of the professional matchmakers are no doubt sincere, there have been several prosecutions of these organizations that have not played by the rules.

At this difficult stage when you may think any solution is better than none, the best advice is to keep your friendships in good repair. Nurture those precious platonic friendships with women you know and respect. Try to get closer to men friends. Cultivate your family too; you may find your own children, for example, can be very supportive, and they often have wisdom beyond their years.

Don't think that your only escape from loneliness will come from another woman. It must come from within yourself, and unless it does your chance of happiness with another person is remote. To go into a new relationship to cure loneliness is an admission that you have passed over the management of your life to someone else. The impulsive "rebound" relationship is rarely successful, simply because it is formed for the wrong reasons. And it starts at a time when our emotional and rational status is, to say the least, questionable.

Loneliness can be managed, and if you recognize that aloneness is a condition that can be not only acceptable but desirable, then you will learn to overcome the unhappy state that we call loneliness and replace it with a state of contentment with your own company. When you have managed to achieve this, you will be amazed how people start to gravitate to you. You will discover the great joy of meeting and responding to new friends and you will wonder why you were not able to attract people when you really needed them. If you stop to consider it, you realize of course that during your negative period you projected a negative image to the world, and even the most sympathetic people prefer winners.

Don't be afraid to talk to your friends, and don't be persuaded that professional help is inappropriate. You may feel that your case is not severe enough to justify consulting a counselor or therapist, but don't dismiss the idea out of hand. You may find that one session with an enlightened professional could change your whole approach to recovery. More importantly you may be introduced to other courses of action such as group therapy, co-counseling or other forms of self-help.

Men unfortunately tend to think of such activities as a sign of weakness. This is a pity because in fact it takes some courage to become involved, and far from indicating weakness it generally implies a degree of personal resolution. There are many such groups, mostly involving both men and women, and my own experience was that they not only opened up vast new horizons for me, but I was able to present some new thoughts to other people too.

Most of all, good friends will always be the best therapy. But remember they are also carrying their own loads of emotional garbage in most cases and you can only expect a certain amount of their time or concentration. Indeed one of the great functions of real friendship is the capacity to listen as well as talk; think of your relationship as being a balanced two-way dialogue. When you reveal yourself to trusted friends you may be astonished at the discovery that they have as much need of your ear as you have of theirs. Most people have some problems and you may find that you are able to help them dramatically by simply listening. And the process of listening can be uniquely therapeutic. This exchange of listening and talking is in fact the basis of the co-counseling movement which is, in my experience, a very valuable form of therapy for some people.

At the end of the day we can only become complete people when we recognize that our loneliness has nothing to do with anybody else. If we are alone and likely to be so for a while, we must learn to make it a positive time. It can be a time for much productive activity in which we can expand our horizons in all directions. It can be a time for intellectual and spiritual development; it can be a time for all kinds of creative activity; and most importantly it can and should be a time for making and nurturing new friendships. By making this time of aloneness fully productive, we are likely to acquire a self-sufficiency that will give us a personal strength we never imagined possible when we were dependent on a partner.

This state of completeness is likely to lead to the point where a future relationship needs to be measured against the possible loss of personal space. If the relationship wins, then you have probably found a wonderful caring, sharing closeness that is likely to last.

ANGER

*To be angry is to revenge the faults
of others upon ourselves.*
Alexander Pope

When a breakup is attended with bitterness and recrimination, as it often is, a predominating feeling of intense anger is not unusual. Men in particular will often translate their sense of rejection and betrayal into violent outbursts of anger. Fortunately these outbursts are more often than not confined to verbal rather than physical actions and will usually be followed by feelings of remorse.

Sometimes, however, the man's anger will be maintained as an ongoing rage and may be directed against his former partner in very frightening ways. This is more likely to be the case where the woman has formed a new relationship. Jealousy is a powerful emotion and can produce very primitive responses from even normally placid men.

I recall a very nasty situation involving a neighbor some years ago when her estranged husband was released from jail and maintained a threatening surveillance of her house. He was careful not to attempt to enter the house, but frequently phoned from a nearby call box and threatened to burn down the house, abduct the children and kill her lover. Although he was a violent man he never carried out the threats, but the mental stress he provoked was unbearable to his wife. At that time there was little she could do to redress the situation; fortunately the law has since been changed to protect people from this kind of harassment.

Sometimes of course the anger gets so far out of control that it does result in physical violence, even murder. We read about these events all too often and wonder at the brutality of men (and occasionally women too) who can so far forget their humanity as to kill or maim a former lover. But I suspect that any man who has been through the misery of an angry split will begin to understand some of the ingredients that lead to this kind of madness. And indeed it is a temporary madness in most cases that brings about this extreme behavior.

When the power of rage is stronger than the bounds of reason, we have a formula for tragedy. If you feel that your anger is reaching uncontrollable levels, don't add to the burden by feeling guilty as well. It is inevitable that anger will emerge as a strong ingredient in the aftermath of many partings. But if you begin to fear the consequences of your anger, it's time to seek help before it is too late to avert disaster.

Help may be best obtained through your family doctor who will possibly refer you to a psychotherapist. Or you may have confidence in one of the many counseling services available. Whatever course you adopt, don't delay taking action. Not only because of possible violence being a consequence, but equally importantly because you will make yourself ill if you allow anger to dominate your life. Anger is a time bomb that, if not defused, could kill someone; and it could be you. There are theories that anger is a major cause of disease, even cancer. At best, prolonged anger will leave you dysfunctional to a greater or lesser extent.

There are a number of books on the subject of anger with some excellent advice about managing and controlling it. These are referred to in the bibliography at the back of this book. If you are afraid that your anger is getting out of control these may be able to help you come to terms with your emotions. You should realize that anger is a normal and even healthy emotion and after a parting you would not be human if you did not have some experience of it. Violence on the other hand is an unacceptable consequence of anger which is out of control. If you have the slightest fear that you may be on the point of committing a violent act, seek help straightaway.

The paradoxical thing about anger is that it damages the angry person more than the object of the emotion. As often as not the other party may be blissfully unaware that he or she is the object of such angry thoughts. It's not until something triggers an actual confrontation that the full extent of the emotion is revealed. And that's the point at which irreversible damage can be done.

Unloading this burden of anger is not easy. It's a hard emotion to shake loose because it attaches itself to the very center of our egos. It is a primitive feeling related to survival. We feel that anger is a reasonable emotion to experience in the circumstances following rejection, betrayal and grief that often accompany a parting. One man I know said of his estranged wife: "I don't hate her. How could I hate her? It's just that I want her to suffer as much pain as I am going through. And I can't forgive her for making me act so totally out of character. I hate feeling so angry and it's not normal for me."

However, we must get rid of this anger if we are to survive and lead lives with some peace in them. Physical activity can help, and particularly with sports that contain an element of aggression. I greatly enjoy playing tennis, and I know a man who mutters a certain lady's name as he slams his power service over the net. He maintains that at the end of a couple of hard sets he almost likes her!

The most useful therapy I have discovered, however, is one suggested to me by a therapist. It comprised the act of writing a letter to the object of my anger in the most frank and uninhibited terms, describing exactly my feelings about her with no holds barred. I wrote a few of these letters and even began to get some sense of achievement out of making them interesting literary pieces. Heaven alone knows what the outcome might have been if they had ever been mailed. As it was, they hurt no one, and they gave me a lot of relief from my anger. I almost felt I could see it dissipating into the atmosphere with the smoke as I burned them—with a kind of ritualistic fervor. It may not work for you, but try it. It worked for me.

I once invited a woman friend to verbalize her anger against her husband, using me as a stand-in. It was eerie watching her whole demeanor change as she warmed to her subject and tore me (him) to shreds with growing violence and evident emotion. I experienced great discomfort in the process, but she told me that it had done her a wonderful amount of good to verbalize the feelings she had been bottling up for a long time. It is a process I can recommend if you are able to find someone who will play the game with you without making you feel foolish. On the other hand you may find it more comfortable to do the exercise using an empty chair.

Managing anger is not something saintly, a turning of the other cheek, so to speak. Anger is a killer emotion and the best reason for getting rid of it is your own self-preservation. Allowed to get out of control, anger can become an all-pervasive sickness and can even lead to acts of uncharacteristic violence.

VIOLENCE

*Marriage is like life in this—
that it is a field of battle
and not a bed of roses.*
ROBERT LOUIS STEVENSON

More often than not there is a state of great emotional tension involved in most partings. Even when there is tacitly a mutual decision about the breakup, at some point it is likely that one or both partners will start to feel bitterness or anger. Sometimes they may have negotiated the big issues and will find that some relatively unimportant thing will lead to arguments, blaming and at worst even violence.

Violence is generally regarded as a male prerogative and most of the media reports we read seem to suggest that men are indeed the worst offenders in this regard. For some men physical violence does seem to be a last-resort weapon. I think it is true to say that men on the whole are less skillful than women in the verbal battles that so often accompany the breakup of a relationship, and can feel driven to acts that may be quite uncharacteristic. It is also well documented that women often use their verbal skills in such a way as to provoke men into violent physical reaction. Men can be very sensitive to taunts or accusations which they feel to be unfair, and in particular respond acutely to any attack on their virility.

It is surprising how many men I know who have been devastated by the accusations of failure as a lover and I wonder whether the accusations are intended more to be inflammatory than a genuine comment on sexual prowess. Either way, a woman who realizes what a vulnerable Achilles' heel a man's sexuality presents has the opportunity to inflict lasting and painful wounds. But she should not be surprised if she gets a reaction out of all proportion to the intended attack.

Jealousy can also produce extreme reaction and I know men whom one would think of as balanced, reasonable people who have admitted to me that jealousy has led them to the brink of violent retribution. In the cases I know both partners were fortunate that some dominant sense of decency (or fear of consequences perhaps?) prevented what might have been dangerous, even fatal, loss of self-control. Again the focus is on the man's sexuality and it seems that this very elemental instinct can be a powerful force when it comes under attack.

Alcohol is well known as a catalyst in situations of potential violence. How often we read of bashings or homicides in which the media reports refer to drinking sessions as a lead-up to violence. I've heard of cases where men about to confront a spouse with some argument associated with separation, will have a couple of drinks to give them Dutch courage. Understandable as it may be, it could be a recipe for an unintentional physical clash. In a situation which could lead to violent outcomes, my advice would be to make sure there is a third party present to offer some restraining influence if things should get out of hand.

Violence is of course not confined to men. Women can be violent given the opportunity and motivation. Many cases are reported of women mutilating men, and once more their motive seems to be almost always sexually oriented. While men are generally stronger physically and thus capable of defending themselves in theory, this is negated in a situation where a woman is armed and he is not. Then again, men have to be careful in defending themselves not to use undue force since this will put them in danger of being open to assault charges or worse.

The ultimate tragedy is when a man is driven to violence and loses control in a blind rage. A man I know was taunted by his estranged wife's accusations that he was no good in bed and was so affected by these attacks that he was unable to consummate his relationship with a new lady with whom he had formed an attachment. On an unscheduled visit to the family home, he found his wife in bed with her new lover and he went berserk, throwing himself on the man and threatening to kill him. When the estranged wife turned on him he threw her across the room, breaking her arm and causing considerable bruising and abrasion. In the confusion the lover escaped and the husband was left to get an ambulance and accompany his wife to hospital. By an odd quirk of fate the episode led to the reunion of the couple for a time and the lover was dismissed. They were all fortunate that the outcome was not more dangerous. He has never forgiven himself for the loss of control that led to this act, as he still sees it, of savagery.

It is easy to stand in judgment of men who become violent in a broken relationship. It should be remembered, however, that most of us, if we care anything for our partners, will feel pain and anger that we may never have experienced before. It is impossible to anticipate how strong our emotions may be and how far they may lead us toward the brink of violence. As I have said elsewhere, any man who feels he is losing control of his emotions to the point where violence is possible should immediately seek counseling. To leave it too long could result in actions that are irreversible and could end in tragedy.

BLAMING

And the best and worst of this is
That neither is most to blame
If you have forgotten my kisses
And I have forgotten your name.
A. C. SWINBURNE

When I did a course in drama writing some time ago, we were told that conflict was the essence of good theater. Be that as it may, conflict in a fractured relationship is a very painful aspect of the parting process—and yes, it does have the elements of theater about it. If you've both been able to preserve a sense of humor it may have overtones of comedy; but more often the conflict and the blaming game will produce heavy drama, even tragedy.

The blaming game is almost a mandatory part of a breakup, it seems. Perhaps it is even one of the fundamental causes of relationships failing. In any case the blaming game can lead to irreparable damage to a relationship and cause untold grief to the participants.

It is a sad and strange phenomenon that causes people who have once loved each other to reach a point of disenchantment where they not only no longer agree but are actively and aggressively hostile to each other. The tragic aspect of the blaming game is that it produces its own players. As the angry dialogues develop, we find ourselves adopting the role our partner is writing for us. Two normally pleasant and considerate people will soon assume the roles of antagonistic baddies and play out their roles with savage intensity.

You soon begin to wonder what happened to that gentle, loving woman you married; and she no doubt is mourning the loss of the caring, sensitive partner who has turned into such a beast. When you play the blaming game it doesn't take long to create a

Greek tragedy. So we must ask where it all begins. Is it that we were always flawed characters and that our mutual recognition of this has only been triggered by the parting? Or are we still fundamentally OK people who are behaving irrationally under the stress of separation?

I prefer to believe the latter is generally the case, and if so there is probably a way of bringing the blaming game into control. To do so we need to recognize a number of things that can be dealt with to take the heat out of our anger. The first of these is that blaming a partner is most likely motivated by one's own sense of guilt; and it is generally agreed that both partners in a breakup will feel some guilt even when one is predominantly responsible. So there is a transference of guilt from one to the other and often the accusations are based on one's own sense of failure. If we are able to stop and consider this possibility we may be able to avert unfair blame from fueling the fires of anger.

Then we should be able to see that both protagonists are the losers in the blaming game. And if there are children involved, they may be the biggest losers of all. Surely no one wants to play a game in which everyone loses.

It's not easy to walk away from the challenge of a well-contested blaming game, but it makes eminently good sense to avoid the open conflict it generally leads to. If you can keep your cool and learn defensive tactics there is a chance that you will be able to deflect the worst of the damage. This is not to suggest that turning the other cheek is appropriate. Rather it means turning the other person's wrath against them. Consider these two brief hypothetical dialogues:

She: The trouble with you is that you don't care for anyone but yourself.
He: If that were true I'd have left years ago.
She: You wouldn't have the guts. You'd be lost without your support system.
He: What support? All I get from you is negligible.
She: If it weren't for me you'd be a hopeless drunk by now.

And so on it goes, getting more and more bitter, more and more irrelevant until eventually both parties explode with rage. Violence is not an impossible consequence.

A possible alternative scenario might sound more like this:

She: The trouble with you is you don't care for anyone but yourself.

He: That's a bit unfair. I'm sorry you feel that way.

She: Well it seems lately you don't care about us at all.

He: I really do care a lot. I've been under a lot of pressure and perhaps I haven't talked enough about it.

She: Why don't you talk? You're so private about your work.

He: You always seem bored by my activities—it's not your responsibility to sort out my business problems.

She: I'd have liked to help but you never asked me.

By admitting one's feelings some of the anger is deflected and instead of the blame escalating into a violent clash, both parties are beginning to feel regret for their own failure to communicate properly. There is perhaps not a solution to the parting, but at least by defensive fighting tactics a reasonably civilized discourse can be maintained.

One of the most infuriating catalysts to a good bout of blaming is the "holier than thou" attitude, which I suspect may be a somewhat male attribute. It is easy to stand on a lofty peak in these arguments and adopt a slightly patronizing attitude. Men are phlegmatic, women are hysterical. We all know that, so let's adopt the archetypal role and be the strong silent man, a Rock of Gibraltar standing steadfastly against the storms of abuse. The lady may be forgiven for wanting to break a chair over your condescending head if you think this is the answer. To treat each other as equals, with respect, and to admit to feelings, is essential to the conduct of a good argument if we are to avoid the severe damage that the blaming game can induce.

Finally, we should acknowledge the need for counseling if it reaches that point. Mediation counseling is available in most places these days and is much better than allowing the argument to become adversarial. That's when the lawyers begin to be the only winners and the couple often end up in a permanent state of bitterness.

FRIENDS

◆◆◆◆◆◆◆◆◆◆◆◆◆

Those friends thou hast, and their adoption tried,
Grapple them to thy soul with hoops of steel.
                                    WILLIAM SHAKESPEARE

When you split up you need to be aware of the effect this will have on your friends. Don't count on too much help from them particularly in the early stages of your new single state. Accept that they may not be able to deal effectively with the new dynamics of your relationship with them.

Several factors may contribute to an awkward attitude on their part and the most important of these is their reluctance to be judgmental. You have no doubt about the causes of the rift and are quite satisfied where the blame lies (or at least most of it). But your friends will be puzzled and confused in their attitude to you and your partner. I can recall discussing with my partner the rights and wrongs of other couples' breakups and finding we had quite strong differences of opinion.

"But she is very argumentative"; "And he's totally unreasonable"; "She's very selfish", "He's mean" and so on. Often the simplest thing is to avoid both parties in the hope that they may get back together again. In any case you don't want to appear to be partial to either, so it's easiest if you leave them alone.

During one period of aloneness I was devastated by what seemed to be the desertion of nearly all our friends. I assumed that they felt more loyalty to my estranged wife than they did to me, but later over dinner with my wife it emerged that she had seen none of them either. There was one exception, and I admired the balance that this woman showed in being able to maintain a friendship with both of us without once betraying any partiality. One man I know said his main concern was with what he called "Trojan horses," friends who maintained contact with him but regularly reported on his activities to his estranged wife.

Even for those friends who are in your corner, there will be limitations to their loyalty and it is important to realize where the bonds extend to. Years ago an ex-partner formed a new relationship and introduced her friend to a couple who were doing their best to be evenhanded. The husband of this couple reported to me what a disgusting little man the new guy was, how uncouth, ill-mannered and generally unacceptable they had found him. It was their last contact with either of us, in part because I had felt compelled to come to his defense, knowing him as a generally very nice man. The fact was that their loyalty, already divided, was being tested beyond its capacity.

Then there is the fear of competition. Although I think this is more a problem for single women than for single men, it can happen. Some husbands may easily feel threatened by the regular contact you may innocently have with their family. In some cases of course they may be justified, since a single man can have romantic connotations for a bored housewife, and close friendships can often be only a step away from something more dangerous. Where there is a strong sympathy for your situation this too can be an ingredient for concern about sustaining a platonic relationship. And I strongly urge the maintenance of a platonic relationship. The last thing you (or anyone else) need is an eternal triangle with all the messy consequences.

On the other hand you may have friends who have lots of single lady friends, and you will be targeted for attempts at matchmaking. I had a good deal of exposure to this treatment at one time and endured some fairly painful evenings in consequence. Mind you I also enjoyed some excellent meals, and often pleasant company.

I recall one memorable evening, however, when I was seated at dinner next to a very beautiful and elegant lady who had clearly been invited to meet me and vice versa. She was intelligent, charming and in every way most desirable. But early in the dialogue she made it clear that she was already in a strong permanent relationship—with a woman of my acquaintance. I appreciated her frankness and we mutually enjoyed the evening without having to speculate on the outcome.

By the same token I did meet a very lovely woman with whom I had a long and loving relationship, in just such circumstances. My hostess was a lady of great perception and told me afterwards that she had hesitated for a long while before bringing us together because she didn't want to be responsible for introducing two of her best friends in case we fell out later and blamed her!

Dinner parties tend to be formal and the obvious designs of a plotting hostess become obvious to everyone. If you can influence your friends, less formal gatherings may be much more constructive—in particular those in which people can move around and preferably where there are numbers of single people. The ever popular cocktail party is not such a bad idea in that regard.

The adage that old friends are best may have some merit but in the single state you may need to challenge the assumption that they are going to remain friends. There is a case for finding a new network of supportive friends when your life changes course. This is not to say that all your old friends will disappear, but it is natural and normal to seek support from people who understand your needs and for whom you too can be supportive. As your situation changes so your circle of friends may also change shape. In particular, if you form a new relationship you will find the dynamics of friendships will change again. Be prepared for new people to enter your new life. It can be a stimulating experience, and will very greatly contribute to your growth.

CELIBACY

*There is much to be said for Mrs Fist—
she is hygienic, never makes scenes,
costs nothing, is utterly
loyal and always at hand
when needed.*
TRUMAN CAPOTE

When you suddenly find yourself without a partner sex is bound to be a problem you will have to face up to . . . or, to be more precise, the lack of sex. Are you to consider, at least for a time, the possibility of leading a celibate life, or are you going to settle for casual sex? There are two very opposed viewpoints about this and you're going to have to consider them.

Celia Haddon in *The Sensuous Lie* asks the question: "Sex—is it fun?—is it natural?—is it even good for you?" and then goes on to explain why it is not fun. Sex, she says, "is merely bodies touching, genitals engaged in each other, a series of movements and sensations that often culminate in orgasm." Well, that isn't so bad, you may say. But she does make a point when she says that the act of sex, in its mechanics, is much the same in a rape as it is in a loving relationship.

The case for casual sex is that it *is* fun; that it can be very comforting; that it can be a great boost to the ego when it is most needed. The proponents for casual sex will say that a deep emotional attachment is not essential to the mutual enjoyment of what is a very natural act. As long as no one gets hurt, they say, go for it.

The first thing to consider when you start to think about this choice is the effect it will have on your own emotions. At this point, if you have only recently separated, you will be feeling very raw emotionally and you may be in a very vulnerable frame of mind. You will need to think about the effect of having this intimate contact with another person when you are still trying to come to grips with all kinds of conflicting feelings. Some men, I know, find regular intercourse almost as vital as regular meals. For them there is presumably a remedy in casual sex, and I think they probably project their need in a way that finds a response from women with similar needs.

Perhaps for many men this casual sexual regime may be the answer, at least in the short term. I am also prepared to believe that it may have more appeal for younger men whose sex drive is at its peak, than it would for more mature men who may have sexually slowed down a little. Whatever the answer I believe that most men in the longer term seek a more fulfilling sex life than "merely bodies touching."

I personally suffer from being what a friend described as "an incurable romantic," which tends to render sex with casual acquaintances, or even good friends, relatively pointless. I also feel that the act of sex is an automatic commitment whether it is expressed or implicit. Sex with a prostitute, for example, is a commitment only to pay for her time and cooperation and to not treat her unkindly. To most women there is generally an expectation of something more than "Wham, bam and thank you, ma'am" after a one-night stand. A young and sensitive student of mine once told me that she had suffered much sadness following the casual relationships she had embarked on for a short time as a teenager while traveling abroad. Now in her twenties, she longs for a deeper relationship and is resolved to remain celibate until she finds it.

If you value your platonic friendships you will do well to avoid taking them further than they are meant to go. It is so easy to spoil a friendship by pressing the sexual needs when they are not reciprocated. And nothing can be more degrading than to accept sexual favors offered in sympathy but without desire.

If you are one of those men who need the magic chemistry to bring a relationship to life then you may suffer some periods of frustration if the right lady is not available. Falling in love is wonderful, but you can't engineer it and love at first sight is largely for Mills and Boon stories I suspect. Sometimes love only develops after a friendship has had time to grow and mature into something more deep. And let's face it, you may have to kiss a lot of frogs before you find one that turns into a princess.

So, if you have decided for the moment to remain at least mildly celibate, how do you cope without a sexual partner? Obviously you will need to face the fact that masturbation is an option if only a temporary one. As one who grew up in a generation which was threatened with blindness, hairy palms and even insanity as a consequence of "self-abuse," I would be the last person to suggest that there is anything wrong with that idea. I remember the story of the researcher who reported that 98 per cent of men admitted to masturbating and that the other 2 per cent were pathological liars! Most of us I suspect no longer try to deny our propensity for auto-eroticism. Indeed I have a friend who claims that it is his preferred practice as he believes he meets a better class of person.

So if we accept that masturbation may be a necessary adjunct to our period of adjustment after a parting, maybe we should also consider what value pornographic material may have. If it turns you on then it may have a valuable place in your recovery. Some pornography is of course so unpleasant that it may be more of a turn-off than a turn-on. I would in particular draw the line at violent material or that which is oriented to child pornography. On the other hand there are magazines and videos which are stimulating, tasteful and often downright good fun. They can and should put our sexuality into proper perspective and make us realize that we are not supposed to be ashamed of eroticism. If romantic love is out of our grasp for the moment let us not throw the baby out with the bathwater. Erotic fantasy is not the complete answer but it's better than nothing.

There is of course a positive side to celibacy which we should not ignore. This relates to the redirection of sexual energy into other activities. Sport and exercise are the more obvious channels, but even more important are intellectual, spiritual and creative activities. The religious orders which require celibacy as a way of life certainly seem to produce a fine aesthetic as well as ascetic concentration of the intellect. It is also a well-documented fact that many great athletes, artists, poets and writers produced their best work during periods of celibacy. My own experience, and that of friends, is that there is a noticeable lift in productive capacity and more sustained concentration when sex is not a distraction.

Every man will need to deal with sexual frustration after a parting as best he can. One man's meat, if one may be forgiven for a bad pun, is another man's poison. Bad sex or casual relationships that cause pain or hurt are worse than none. If you are in a fragile state of mind anyway, you may not be able to cope with any kind of additional stress even if it does provide some transient comfort. And in this age of AIDS and other nasty sexually transmitted diseases casual sex needs to be treated with care and responsibility.

SURVIVAL

*Alas! the love of women! it is known
To be a lovely and a fearful thing!*
LORD BYRON

We may not wish to be reminded of this—but we are all the products of a woman's influence in our childhood. For most men the early environment was distinctly matriarchal and for many of us the female influence may well have continued into adulthood.

For most of us our first and most intimate moments started at our mother's breast. With rare exceptions our mothers, and possibly aunts and grandmothers as well, were our most constant and strongest influence through our formative years. It's not surprising that most of us have become dependent on women.

For many men the transition from adolescence to manhood is marked only by a change of the female minder. Those of us who married young found no problem in accepting a wife's influence as we relinquished our mother's. Some men actually move from one female-dominated environment to another without the usual period of bachelor living. Even those who did have some single-life experience often maintained a strong lifeline with mother or some other carer.

The winds of change are blowing, but I think most men facing separation are ill prepared for the single state in both emotional and practical terms. We simply have never been taught the skills we need to lead fulfilling lives on our own without a partner.

But it's never too late to learn, and we must learn if we are to make the single existence tolerable. We must learn the basic living skills first so that we can remain healthy. Some rudimentary knowledge of dietary matters is good, and if you've never been a cook, now is the time to discover some culinary delights of your own invention. I have never been obsessed with kitchen activities and would still prefer to dine out if money were no object. But I have nevertheless acquired some skills and have a small repertoire of dishes which comes under the "tried and trusted" category. I even have guests for dinner sometimes and have a sneaking satisfaction in seeing empty plates, particularly those of women guests who may have been inclined to consider me somewhat helpless in the kitchen.

Aside from these practical matters, men also, I believe, have another fundamental problem. It relates to the incapacity to deal with their personal feelings in the way that most women seem to be able to. Women are more prepared to share their feelings with other women and with certain men friends. Most of the men I know, with a couple of sensitive exceptions, can't do this with their male friends. We are expected to be too tough to admit we are bleeding.

I overheard a dialogue in a bar one night between two ordinary men, which I think graphically demonstrates this tough guy attitude. They had both clearly been recently separated from their wives and both were obsessed with the need to reveal no sign of weakness or distress. The dialogue, as far as I can remember, went something like this:

A: How ya doing, buddy?
B: Good. Good. Real good.
A: Seen Shirl lately?
B: Yeah, the cranky bitch.
A: Still on yer back then, is she?
B: Never lets up. Gimme, gimme all the time. Maintenance, custody, property hassles, letters from the lawyers every week.
A: Tell me about it! I'm copping the same thing. They're all the same. If they didn't have . . .
B: Yeah, I know, we'd throw stones at them.
A: Are you missing her?
B: Shit, no. I'm glad she's gone. It's just she can't let go. And what she's doing to the kids gets to me. They don't deserve

A: Still with the boyfriend then is she?
B: Yeah, the asshole. Reckon he's put her up to a lot of this you know.
A: How's your love life, sport? Getting any?
B: Bloody knocking it back.
A: Anyone special? I mean, I'm not prying, but a man needs a bit.
B: Oh she's special all right. Really loves it. I mean, who needs a cold fish like Shirl when there's all those great babes out there begging for it.
A: Still, Shirl was something else, wasn't she?
B: *Was* is the operative word. I don't want to hear her name again.
A: Sorry, pal. Have another beer?
B: No thanks. Gotta go. It's my weekend for the kids. Darned if I know what I'm going to do with them.
A: Well, good luck, buddy. Keep your pecker up.
B: Jeez! Would you like to rephrase that?

I believe what I was really hearing from B was something like this:

I'm struggling to survive. Shirl is being very aggressive and I'm lonely, hurt and very jealous. It distresses me that her arguments are hurting the kids. And I miss her. My girlfriend is not a substitute. I bet her guy doesn't love her like I used to. I am mortified when I think of him making love to her. I'd rather she was dead. It would be easier to deal with that way. All I have is the kids and I don't know what to say to them.

What a tragedy it is that most men are unable to really say what they mean. Bar talk would be a lot more interesting for a start, and men would be a lot healthier. The two men in the bar were clearly close friends and obviously needed the friendship as a support mechanism. Yet neither was able to relax enough with the other to admit the truth of the pain that was hurting them. For heaven's sake, if you have a good friend load him with your unhappiness. You'll find that he will be enormously flattered that you have enough regard for him to want to tell him. You probably won't get a lot of practical advice but you will sure as hell feel better for relieving yourself of the burden of secrecy with which most of us surround our emotional disasters. Women are fortunate in being able to talk to their girlfriends, and I understand they often have a good cry on a friendly female shoulder.

In fact I have often been the recipient of such confidences from women friends and I like to think I have been able to give them some comfort. So why is it so hard for men to talk to other men? I'm sure it's only a conditioning that has been imposed on us in our Western society, and it's time we stood up and asked for a new set of rules. It could even be possible to get society to acknowledge that it is not only OK for boys to cry if they are really hurting, but it's very unhealthy for them not to.

HOUSEKEEPING

◆◆◆◆◆◆◆◆◆◆◆◆◆

*A man in the house is worth
two in the street.*
MAE WEST

For men who remain in the family home after a breakup, much of what I say here will not apply. Speaking from my own experience and that of friends, the most common trend seems to be for the man to leave, whether or not he is the instigator of the move. For those men the move to a bachelor pad may be quite an experience, possibly one mixed with apprehension and some excitement about the adventure implicit in such a plan.

When you move into your new place you may think of it as a temporary staging camp. If you do you'll probably settle for something cheap and possibly nasty. If you're typical of most men starting again on the single life, you'll be watching your overheads carefully and be prepared to accept something a bit substandard. This is a mistake in my opinion, which you are likely to regret.

In the first place, if my experience is a guide, you'll be there a lot longer than you expect. And anyway, no matter how brief the stay, a depressing environment is the last thing you need at a time when your spirits are likely to be at a low ebb. My advice is to spend a bit of time finding something compatible and, if not luxurious, at least sunny and dry. There is nothing so depressing as a damp cold place.

I made the mistake of securing an apartment on my departure which was the most cheerless, characterless place I have ever lived in. Although at first appearance it was comfortable and modern and in a good neighborhood, it transpired to be cold, sunless and depressing, with a smell like an old tomb. One of my spiritually aware friends used to get quite spooked out by what she thought were sinister vibes. It was a roof over my head, but it gave me no pleasure to live in and left me with a greater degree of depression than I deserved. When I later moved to a pleasant place with a sunny aspect and a spectacular view, my spirits took a huge leap upwards. Significantly, the rent was the same for both places.

Resist the temptation to grab the first "cheapy" and spend time finding something you feel comfortable in. You're probably dropping back a few notches in your living standard as it is, so don't add to your sense of deprivation by saddling yourself with a bad environment at the outset.

I also believe it is very important for your self-esteem to make your place as attractive as you can, given that you probably have budget constraints. Even if you don't plan on entertaining at home it is vital that you make yourself feel welcome. Remember that you are on your own and you can do anything you want in the way of furnishing your place to reflect your individual character. Even a few essential pieces of furniture can be chosen and arranged to project an air of comfort, and there's no need to spend a lot of money. Garage sales, if you can come to terms with that kind of trade, can produce surprising bargains.

The other thing you can do to maintain self-esteem is to be a good housekeeper. It doesn't mean turning into a hyperscrupulous neat freak, but having your place tidy and clean will give you a sense of well-being out of all proportion to the effort required to achieve it. I even tend to get some pleasure out of washing and ironing, a chore that I had at first found degrading and time-wasting. I sometimes think that being well turned out may almost be a gesture of defiance to the female world out there who don't believe you are capable of doing it!

Finally, it is important that you cultivate good eating and drinking habits. I found at first that there was a tendency to drink one or two more glasses than normal in the evening while I was procrastinating about preparing a meal. I find now that by being a bit more rigid about mealtimes I limit my alcohol intake and enjoy my own rather indifferent cooking more. I have also made myself a rule not to drink after dinner at night except in a social situation.

I have referred elsewhere to the desirability of gaining dietary information to help maintain a balanced food intake. As a part of the good housekeeping practice this will help in deciding the right stuff to buy when you're shopping and give you an insight into new alternatives in the culinary mix. I grew up in a family which tended to accept the "meat and two vegs" formula and having lived with a great chef for a while I have discovered what a spectrum of options are open to even the pedestrian cook.

I know a number of bachelors who are superb cooks and I envy but do not attempt to emulate them. I nevertheless have a small repertoire of acceptable dishes and take more pride in making them work than I used to. I seem to have developed a need to impress not only my guests but also myself with food skills that were not hitherto evident. Incidentally I am told that cooking classes are a very good way to meet new friends and also of course are likely to provide you with some good meals along with new skills.

Good housekeeping is, in my belief, an essential ingredient in the formula for survival and growth as a single person. You may well be surprised, as I was, to discover that you actually start to enjoy the art of entertaining at home.

DIVERSIONS

◆◆◆◆◆◆◆◆◆◆◆◆◆◆◆◆◆◆◆

I too will something make
And joy in the making.
ROBERT BRIDGES

I suspect that people with creative skills may be better able to mend their lives than others for whom these gifts may seem alien. To paint a picture, to write a poem, to sing a song; these are certainly diversions that for anyone with the skills and inclinations will be fulfilling activities that will help greatly to draw attention away from loneliness.

To those men who proclaim they can't draw a straight line or sing a note, I suggest they re-examine their skills and inclinations before they opt for a steady diet of television. With the accessibility of low-cost adult education, your single state may present you with a golden opportunity to acquire new skills or improve on old ones. Among my friends and acquaintances several have found very satisfying diversions with all kinds of activities: voice training, art classes, cabinetmaking, upholstery and a host of other interesting things to which in most cases they have become dedicated.

Most of us it seems have at some time had to pass up activities we enjoyed because of the responsible pursuit of being a family provider. This could be your great opportunity to learn something fulfilling and even materially rewarding. Aside from the satisfaction that acquiring skills can produce, the act of learning can be a big morale booster when self-esteem may be at a low ebb.

The other very beneficial aspect of this kind of program is the fact that you will be meeting other people with similar interests. The opportunity to develop new friendships is obvious and the fact that there are shared interests makes it probable that there will be a much higher degree of compatibility than you would expect in a random meeting. The possibility of ultimately forming a relationship is not to be overlooked either.

The adult education courses available in most areas are an excellent way to get started on a learning curve. They are generally not too demanding either of time or concentration, but at the same time can provide good levels of skill development in a friendly social climate. Shared interests, as I have said, are likely to induce friendships of some value and even more importantly, the opportunity is there to meet people who are probably right outside your previous circles. This in itself can be a great experience for someone whose social boundaries have been constrained by narrower levels of contact.

The act of learning is of itself therapeutic. As we seek to expand the horizons of our creative or intellectual worlds we tend to dump off some of the garbage of the past to make room for the new intake of knowledge. We find as we become more and more engrossed with our learning process that we have less and less time or inclination to dwell on our unhappy situations. It forces us to live in the here and now and it generates a healthy and confident expectation of the future. My own experience of several courses has been extraordinarily rewarding in both its psychological benefits and its social implications. I have formed several lasting friendships out of these activities and am now getting much satisfaction from teaching.

Working with our hands is a very primitive instinct and those of us who have been deprived of manual work need a substitute. Gardening, chopping wood and such activities are good but probably not enough to satisfy the need to do something significant with our hands. Pottery, sculpture, carpentry and those kinds of creative manual activities are good for the soul as well as being useful skills. Sometimes the acquisition of such "hobby" skills lead to a desire for further training and even to a whole new career path. I remember a well-known painter some years ago whose career started with his introduction to art by a therapist after he had had a severe flying accident.

Manual activity tends to make time pass quickly and to keep the mind absorbed. If you are trying to forget someone, this beats anything I know for producing controlled amnesia!

Some people find amateur theater or musical groups good activities. There is a sense of urgency about such activities that appeals to some people as the buildup to public performance provides a surge of adrenaline. But by the same token these commitments can be very inflexible and you will need to make sure they are not too intrusive on your life.

Sport too can be a wonderful diversion to bring you out of your moods of despondency. Exercise is essential to our sense of well-being and if you give this another dimension with the addition of social overtones, then that has to be very positive. Tennis was a game from which I used to derive great pleasure, and I'm sure much benefit because of the social environment. Tennis clubs which encourage mixed membership are excellent in this regard, particularly when they also extend the social activities beyond the court. If you are still experiencing residual anger after a parting, tennis can be great for relieving the tension. Belting the daylights out of yellow balls can be rewarding and some people I know actually mutter the name of an estranged partner as they smash a ball down the court. Perhaps that's a little extreme.

Aerobics and gym workouts can be good for stress reduction and it's important for your mental health to feel good about your body as well. A feeling of physical well-being does wonders for the self-esteem. Whatever kind of activity or activities you choose to adopt make sure you use them as a positive part of your growth process. Don't think of your new interest as an escape route . . . think of it as a pathway to new worlds rather than an escape from the old one.

MARKETING

*Wise men ne're sit and wail their loss
But cheerly seek how to redress their harms.*
WILLIAM SHAKESPEARE

I'd like to have five dollars for every time I've heard a man swear, after a breakup, that he'd never again let another woman in his life. It's a statement that comes from the heart, but generally it's a temporary one. In due course they start to be seen in smart gear, and if they can afford it the family sedan is replaced by something a bit more sporty.

They may not admit it but they are prospecting for a new lady. A marriage counselor friend calls it marketing. And indeed that's what it is; smarten up the product, revamp the packaging, check out the target market and get on with the promotional plan.

Clearly this is good positive stuff and is a lot more to be encouraged than the alternative which is often a miserably reclusive life pattern and sometimes a jaundiced attitude to the opposite sex. But now is the time to take careful stock of our real needs and desires.

It's a time to decide what we are really seeking in a relationship. Is it love, friendship, sex, support, or a combination of these; or simply a vague idea that it's not healthy to live alone?

Before you answer that advertisement from the "warm friendly outgoing lady seeking sensitive mature man etc." pause long enough to seriously ask yourself why you want a relationship, and indeed if you are ready to think about starting one. By all means drop in to the singles bars if that turns you on. My own experience was that they were very depressing as a rule and somewhat unrewarding. I recall an occasion with a friend who had had a parting at about the same time as mine had occurred, in a bar which was said to enjoy a strong patronage from lonely and beautiful people. Against my better advice he struck up a hopeful dialogue with a girl who was clearly not very interested, but nevertheless accepted several rounds of drinks from us. He was mortified when she was joined by her friend and presumably lover—an older woman. They left together arm in arm without a backward glance. The experience would have been funny if it weren't for the fact that it did a lot of damage to his ego, and left him feeling very depressed.

I do know people who have made lasting friendships and even good loving relationships through these kinds of meetings or through the lonely hearts advertisements. But on the whole I think there are better ways to implement a marketing campaign. Meeting women in other environments may give you an opportunity to be more discriminating and without the need for an overt commitment up front. It's worth considering too, why the ladies in the ads and the bars are there in the first place. If they are as desperately lonely as you are, do you really think they can help you solve your problems?

I believe a very good strategy is to join groups which interest you for their own sake. Sport, music, theater, debating, dancing . . . you name your own choice of activity. I once joined a choir during a very lonely period of my life and found it to be one of the most enriching experiences in terms of close companionship I have ever enjoyed. In the year or so that we spent as a group I made several real friends of both sexes. Although no romantic connections came from the association, I learned the value of worthwhile platonic friendships. The singing was also good for the soul and a strong bonding developed through the common interest in music. We should not overlook the opportunity to develop friendships with people of both sexes in the working environment. These encounters can be very rewarding, not only because of the intrinsic need for having someone to confide in, but it is sometimes good to have friends who are aware of your problems and may be better able to help in supporting you at work.

Platonic friendships, for the cynics, do exist. It is not only possible but very delightful to share the confidences of a woman who is not defensive of your sexual intentions. Women have a capacity for deep friendships and are often able to give very real and practical support in a way that even close men friends are generally unable to do. I think most men need this kind of friendship of women, but we're not good at generating it. Pride, shyness, fear of rejection or some other perception will often prevent us from reaching out to a woman, and she in turn may well interpret our reluctance as lack of interest.

By the same token there are many women who are too suspicious of a man's motives to allow him close enough to be a real friend. There is a persistent belief on the part of many women that "men are only interested in one thing." And we all know what that is! But things are gradually changing, praise the Lord. Let the winds of change blow free.

A man who is lucky enough to find real friendship with a woman, or with women, is going to find it much easier to get through the trauma of separation and to ultimately find a long-term loving relationship . . . if that's what he really wants. Which raises the question of what kind of relationship you are really seeking. We tend to think of marriage as the norm, or a de facto version which today is seen as much the same thing by many people. But there are other options and they need to be addressed. Some of them are discussed in the next chapter.

SINGLES SCENE

ABSOLUTELY THE BEST EVER For Ladies and Gents (over 25) Sat July 24. Dance. Paddington Fri July 30. Dinner. City CALL JOHN ON Complimentary Newsletter

AMIGOS! No party tonight. Next house party Sat. 31/7. Next Rock 'n' Rumba Sat 14/8.

ATTENTION. SOPHISTICATED SINGLES Join us for mid week madness at our APRES SKI PARTY (sans snow). Wednesday. 28th July. 7.30 p.m Elizas Brasserie. Bay St. Double Bay. Cost $25. Dress: Best apres ski gear. Includes comp. Gluwein and light supper. Great music (D.J.). Bookings essential. Discounts available. For information and bookings call Linnea on

Cocktail Party
Sat. 24th, 8 p.m - 1 a.m $15. People 25 to 39 years of age. Come along and have a great time meeting new people in a friendly relaxed atmosphere, with music, dancing and appetisers. We are expecting over 200 people Dress reg collar and tie, no jeans.

DINNER WITH A DIFFERENCE.
ROUND TABLE 6
All ages welcome. P'matta area. Weekly. Guys and Gals 30-40 needed Ring for details of our dining out club.

HOUSE PARTY Circus Theme Saturday 24 July Join us for all the fun of the fair Luxury apartment with spectacular harbour views. Good food and wine included. Numbers limited and bookings essential. $30. Ph. Robert

OUT AND ABOUT SINGLES FOR THE OVER 30's One of the largest Singles organisations in Sydney's South. with over 2000 ladies and gentlemen listed from all areas. Functions include: House Parties. BBQs. Dinner Dances. Weekends Away, etc. For complimentary Newsletter send S.A.E. to P.O. Box 158. Caringbah 2229 or phone Carol.

SINGLE SCENE. We have weekly parties and functions for men and women, aged 18 to 50. Please call Melissa for further info on

SINGLES. Over 40, enjoy great buffet dinners and good company. Sat. evenings, private home (harbour views). $30 drinks inclusive. BOOKINGS ESSENTIAL. Phone Lynnette on

SOCIAL DINERS
POSITIVE SINGLE PEOPLE The Burning Log Restaurant Dinner/Dance 31st July 80 people attend each function Bookings essent.

TABLE FOR 8
EXPAND your SOCIAL HORIZONS! DINE OUT at top City RESTAURANTS with ARTICULATE people who are DISCERNING but NOT BORING! Men aged 40-55 in demand! PHONE Suzanne
BETWEEN 10.30 TO 6. MONDAY TO FRIDAY

These classified advertisements in a leading daily newspaper [from which the numbers have been deleted] suggest one possible course of action for the lonely male who is into marketing. I haven't tried this method myself but I hear that it can have its rewards for the persistent.

OPTIONS

*Let us not throw the rope
after the bucket.*
CERVANTES

We live in an age when conventional marriage is no longer the only option for a permanent relationship. In fact many people would consider the idea of living together almost as a necessary prelude to marriage if not a permanent alternative. A couple I know who have lived together for many years told me that they are scared of getting married in case it changes something they believe to be very good as it is. This philosophy of "if it ain't broke, don't fix it" is I think fairly widespread, and we have all heard of the cases of people who have parted after marriages that follow long and happy relationships.

If you are really exploring the options thoroughly, perhaps it is not a bad idea to look at even the quite unconventional ones before you decide to conform. There are so many possibilities if you are prepared to think outside the conventional parameters.

One of the more unusual relationships I have known was a genuine *ménage à trois*—husband, wife and wife's lover who shared a house along with the child of the marriage. She grew into a beautiful and well-adjusted young woman with children of her own who seem to be equally well adjusted. Despite the fact that "society" of the day may have seen the arrangement as unconventional or even bizarre, I believe the little girl was fortunate in growing up in an environment in which she was secure in the knowledge that she was well loved by three caring people.

This story simply demonstrates the fact that it is possible to think about alternatives other than conventional marriage. Most of us probably wouldn't be comfortable with a *ménage à trois* arrangement, but many successful relationships are built on the decision to live in separate places and to adopt an agreed pattern of visits. One man I know decided to move into a small apartment near the family home so he could combine his strong need for personal space with a very genuine love for his wife and children. I believe it works well for them all. Clearly one would need the income to allow for this increase in basic overheads.

A lady of my acquaintance was the "mistress" for many years of a distinguished and wealthy man who built her a house near his own in a select suburb. He spent his nights with her but had his own very elegant bachelor home in which he entertained extensively. He was of the old school which set great importance on the appearance of things, and he maintained the dual life essentially to protect the lady's reputation. This was an era in which people were concerned with such things, and it was even said that he always arrived and departed from her house in darkness to protect her from scandal! The story has an almost Victorian royalty flavor about it. When he died he willed her a large fortune and she told me she had had an ideally happy relationship based on great affection and trust, that lasted over twenty years.

With the attitudes of today's society so much more liberal than they were in those days the options are many and varied. We really don't need to settle on conventional marriage the second time around. Indeed for many couples the traditional marriage commitment can be a serious inhibition to establishing a good bonding. For some people it can mean simply a set of imposed regulations with no bearing on the wishes or the needs of the couple. There is something to be said for rules that are made and agreed by the couple. I refer to this again in the chapter titled Contracts.

Probably a lot of people go into marriage simply because it is the convention, and may never have considered the alternatives. I know in my case that the options never occurred to me as viable when I was widowed after twenty years of happy marriage. My real desire as I now realize, was to try to duplicate my first marriage as far as I could. There were also the considerations of the desire for social acceptability expected by my new in-laws and for the provision of a stable environment for my children. Sadly neither of these needs was permanently met because the marriage foundered, largely I suspect because of the false premise on which it was initiated.

In exploring the many options available to a couple in the process of bonding, the one golden rule is that the chosen style is totally acceptable to both parties. Concern for the feelings of outsiders should be very secondary, because if it is not right for the couple it won't be right for anybody else. Clearly the interests of children must be of great moment, but we need to remember that children in today's society are accustomed to the unconventional, and their peers are unlikely to discriminate against them because of out-of-the-ordinary family formations.

The purpose of exploring this question of options is simply to allow men contemplating a new relationship to stop for a moment and consider what is likely to be best for them and their partner. I'm sure most people fail to really discuss the options in a frank and full manner, and it is so important to do so. Above all keep reminding yourself that your new relationship will not be a bit like the last one, so don't try to duplicate it or you will face awful disappointment. Be prepared, particularly if you have had a long and happy relationship over many years, to abandon some of your convictions and preconceived ideas. A younger woman may want to introduce you to all kinds of new concepts, and if you want to be happy you will need to listen well!

If your new lady has children be very sure what is implied in stepparenting. Bringing up someone else's children requires a very special kind of compassion and sensitivity. Even in a "normal" marriage the influence of children can be dangerously disruptive to the parents' relationship. For a stepfather there are many difficulties in steering through the shoals in the waters of an inherited family. I have more to say about this in another chapter.

COUNSELING

Take my counsel happy man;
Act upon it if you can!
　　　SIR W. S. GILBERT

In his book *Single Fathers*, John Wilson quotes the findings of a study he undertook to determine what resources men found most helpful in their adjustment to their single-father roles. Self-help rated at the top of the list, and religious organizations were at the bottom.

To generalize, it clearly emerged that family/friendship-based support rated as much more helpful than formal services provided by social service or voluntary organizations. This very much confirmed my own experience and that reported by friends. It is significant that Wilson's study showed "Helping myself" as the most significant influence by far.

My own belief is that growing through the process of parting will primarily come from within ourselves. In the main we have to deal with bringing about the changes that are essential to our recovery. Nevertheless the help and support of friends are very necessary. We do need this network if only to have someone tell us we are worthwhile people.

Good friends, however, no matter how well intentioned, may not be the best counselors, even those who have had experience of broken relationships. You may be subjected to a plethora of platitudes from people who really don't know how to advise you properly.

Most of my friends kept reassuring me that it would be OK in time and that my problems would be solved by (a) meeting a new lady, (b) going on a trip or (c) the passing of time. They all had good advice to offer and their cheerful acceptance of the situation did nothing to reduce my personal misery.

Almost all of my friends assumed that my greatest need was to form another relationship as soon as possible. The idea of being alone was generally seen as unnatural and something to be remedied as soon as the suitable partner came into view. There was one man with a different view and I'm glad I listened to him. He urged me to accept aloneness as a first step to recovery. It was good advice; it is of course the thrust of much of what I say in this book. He himself had come to the end of his second marriage at an age when he was wise enough to take stock of his life. He was able to demonstrate to me how full and happy a life he was able to lead in his celibate state. He told me how productive he had become and how the sadness of parting had been lessened by his new-found freedom. Like me, he had spent all his adult life in a husband/father role and this sudden release of personal energy was a revelation.

Friends are wonderful and vital to our recovery process, but their role should be supportive rather than instructional. Listen to their experiences because you will learn much about human nature. A lot of what you hear may be useful in the negative sense—a kind of "there but for the grace of God go I" because of which you may be able to avoid other people's pitfalls. It is particularly good to have people you can call when you are really down. The telephone has been my lifeline, and many friends have helped me out of the deep pit simply by being on the end of the phone. Often our dialogue was unrelated to my situation—just a friendly chat.

I often wonder in retrospect if some of my friends may have scratched their heads after one of these talks and said, "What was that all about?" In case there is anybody out there nodding, let me say it was about survival, it was about sanity.

As to professional counseling, there is much to be said for that kind which deals with specifics. It doesn't make a lot of sense to take your car to the mechanic and simply say that it's not running too well. If you can point to sloppy steering, a noisy muffler or poor starting, you're likely to get a more immediate and effective repair job. My lay opinion is that we need to take the same attitude to obtaining good counseling. Be specific about the nature of your need for counseling and I suspect you will derive great benefit from it.

Here is a list of things that you may feel need addressing in specific terms. You may have several of these problems at once or they may occur serially; or you may have only one or two that are strong enough to justify attention: anger, grief, depression, fear, jealousy, uncertainty, poor sleep patterns, poor appetite, impotence, aggression, memory loss, pains, skin disorders; the list could go on, but you will know instinctively what especially ails you. My approach was to actually write down my own diagnostic parameters something like this:

"I am sleeping fitfully and wake up with heart palpitations. I am suffering intermittent fits of acute depression. My concentration is not good."

My first port of call would be to my family doctor. It is of course possible that he or she may prescribe pills to alter your moods and this may be appropriate in some cases, at least in the shorter term. I personally would be seeking more profound and longer-term help and your family doctor is the best person to recommend the most suitable kind of therapy for your needs. He or she will no doubt be familiar with all the services available in your district, and the more enlightened will also be aware of any new-age/alternative treatments that may be helpful. These could include such things as tai chi, yoga, rebirthing, meditation, co-counseling and other methods which you may find helpful in assisting your growth in this difficult time.

As to the more conventional therapies there has been a great deal of progress in recent years. Those who have been exposed to the slightly hit or miss procedures of a couple of decades ago will be pleased to know that there is a great deal more professionality in these areas today. My own recollection of marriage guidance counseling a long time ago was enough to make me chary of repeating the experience. The lady who had been assigned to my case, and whom I assumed to be just a well-meaning do-gooder, transpired to be an avid voyeur, and clearly got her thrills vicariously from the sexual descriptions of her clients. I was unkind enough to terminate our relationship by describing a highly creative series of bizarre practices which nearly sent the poor lady into a frenzy.

My more recent experience is of highly trained professionals working in this field today, almost all apparently graduates with psychology skills, and mostly people with a lot of compassion. Professional counseling may well be your road to full and speedy recovery and is worth investigating. Although, as I have suggested already, the recovery process will come mainly from your own efforts, some help is desirable. A flesh wound will certainly recover unaided in due course, but medication and dressing will accelerate the process. The wounds of a parting, too, will respond to special care.

STEREOTYPES

My manhood long misled by wandering fires
Followed false lights; and when their glimpse was gone
My pride struck out new sparkles of her own.
JOHN DRYDEN

In coming to terms with their emotions, one of the greatest inhibitions men have is that of conforming to the accepted male stereotype. They find it hard to move away from their macho, tough-guy role. Probably born of our pioneer ancestry, the image has been perpetuated by our balladists, by our legends and by contemporary stars. It's a tough set of acts to follow and almost denies the possibility of living out the SNAGS (Sensitive New Age Guys) philosophy without attracting attention of the unwelcome kind.

In times of stress associated with a broken relationship most of us have a desperate desire to talk about it with someone sympathetic. Women have no problem talking to other women and it seems to have a significant effect on their recovery. Men generally are unable to talk to their male friends and certainly few men are able to talk at the totally uninhibited level that is needed to unload the pangs of grief. To have another man cry on your shoulder (literally) is an experience that all but the most sensitive will abhor. It did in fact happen to me once during a group therapy session, and I found myself rocking this retired soldier in my arms while he sobbed his heart out about his wife's desertion.

In any other situation than a group therapy one, I think we would both have felt total embarrassment and would undoubtedly have been regarded with some suspicion by our peers. But that's how our society views the male stereotype and it's likely to change little across the spectrum of society despite the New Age. Sadly the heterosexual male is trapped by his stereotype, and sensitivity will be equated by his peers as something verging on the effeminate if not actually homosexual. Tell us as often as you like that we all have a feminine side to our makeup; most of us are damned if we're going to let anyone see it!

Given that intimate and healing communication with other men is largely impossible, we are likely to turn to women as our confidantes. But therein lies a tangled web—at least potentially. Platonic friendships with women are certainly possible and as I have suggested can be very rewarding. But the intimacy of self-revelation can easily lead to expectations of a closer relationship. Then there is the problem of jealousies which may stand in the way of an intimate level of communication. There can be a further inhibition in that a man may hesitate to discuss his problems with a woman who may feel it is her right or even duty to discuss it with her husband.

In an article about male dependence, Bettina Arndt, says, "His wife becomes his lifeline because of the barriers that prevent men from being intimate with each other and the jealousies that stop them becoming friends with other women." How sadly true, particularly for a man who suddenly finds himself alone after half a lifetime attached to the same spousal lifeline.

Thus many men are left with little alternative but to tough it out on their own, or to seek professional counseling. The latter is unfortunately seen by many men as useless and such is the attitude to psychiatrists and other mental health professionals that many people of both sexes refuse to involve them. In a survey quoted elsewhere a group of men in the study put talking to friends at the top of their counseling experiences. We really do need to break down the stereotype barriers and learn to talk openly to our friends. Women are almost always good listeners in my experience and if your circle of women friends is limited don't be afraid to talk to work colleagues. I have also been surprised at the wise counsel I have received from men once I was able to breach the barrier of male reserve on both sides. Particularly if you talk to men who have been through the same kind of experience as you are in, you'll be rewarded with the sympathy you tap into.

And if you're saying that sympathy isn't normal from another man—brother, you'd better believe it. There are lots of compassionate men out there if you seek them out and relax your own reserve.

Part Two
GROWING

BEGINNINGS

Come live with me and be my love
And we will all the pleasures prove.
CHRISTOPHER MARLOWE

You will know when you have come to the end of your old love. When you can finally think of her without your heart palpitating; when you can see her passing by without feeling anger or sadness; when you really don't care who she is sleeping with—then you are free!

Now you can think about a new relationship if you want one. Now you can start looking at other women in a more speculative way; not as potential carers but as companions with equal rights and privileges, with the possibility that you may at some time ask them to share your life. You are likely now to meet lots of interesting people, and you may find that many of the women you have already met start to take on a new meaning for you. You will probably find too that old friends will start to treat you differently, more as an interesting companion than as someone needing support. It is a good feeling, this sense of being whole. It means the end of an era and the beginning of new beginnings.

Make this a joyful voyage of discovery. Let the world know you are somebody worthwhile with a purpose in life and a desire to share the good things. This could be one of the most exciting times in your life if you allow yourself the great pleasure of relating to other people without reserve or constraint. Remember you are presenting yourself to others as yourself; you are no longer 50 per cent of a relationship. Let them know that what they see is what they get!

By the same token, be discerning about the people you meet. You can have fun trying to assess their potential attraction to you. Think about the things you like about them as well as the things that irritate you. Make this a time when you really can decide not to worry about what people think of you. Instead think about whether you can be bothered to cultivate their friendship. You'll be surprised how often you'll find that some of the initially attractive people turn out to be quite boring on closer acquaintance. But there will be one or two who leave a residual impression and you will want to follow up some of these chance meetings with another opportunity to talk.

But don't rush it! If you meet a woman who appeals to you and you feel there is a mutual attraction, you don't have to pounce on her to let her know how you feel. Conversely if she pounces on you too eagerly it may be wise to take a step backwards and count to ten before you start making commitments. If you consummate a relationship before it's ready to be agreed on it can be difficult to take it back to something platonic. Low-key approaches can be seen too as showing sensitivity as indeed they do. Perhaps a film for starters—but check the nature of the program first. There's some pretty lurid stuff about and it can be embarrassing to sit through two hours of soft-core porn with a lady you've just met and who turns out to be unimpressed with copulation as a spectator sport.

Candlelit dinners are fine but they can easily create a costly precedent. It's important early in a new relationship not to create any false impressions, and if you are big-noting with occasions you can't sustain you may end up with a disappointed partner later on when you have to admit to champagne tastes with a beer income. If this is to be the beginning of a long-term relationship, then it is important that all your communication should be honest and direct. Good communication is the very cornerstone of a relationship and it should start on day one. Spare her the bullshit; let her know who you really are, warts and all. If it's a picture she doesn't like, it's better that she knows now than later on when she can say with some justification that you have changed. Likewise this direct approach will also make it easy for her to reveal who she really is and how she feels.

As the friendship progresses it may be appropriate to exchange views about the rules of the relationship to be if it seems to be going that way. A marriage counselor once told me that he thought the main problem in present-day marriages was the fact that there was no longer a rule book. He meant of course that there was little regard any more for the old rules laid down in the Christian marriage ceremony. People used to be comfortable with the guidelines that took them right from the altar to the grave with the "till death us do part" philosophy, and now there are no guidelines to replace this credo. While many marriages are still performed with the old rites, there is only a small minority of people who treat them seriously. Once we knew when we were breaking the rules!

His advice to couples contemplating marriage or entering a long-term relationship is to write their own rule book. For some people the old biblical lines may be close to their needs and for other couples a more relaxed code may be better. There is more about this in a chapter called Contracts. Meanwhile at the courtship stage (a lovely old-fashioned word!) there should be a lot of uninhibited talking. This should establish as much about each partner as possible, even to the point of revealing some very private feelings. Honesty and clear communication can go a long way towards charting the shoals on which a marriage can founder. Even the possible destruction of a relationship before it starts is better than the discovery too late of some fundamental obstacle to mutual happiness.

There was a tragic case I learned of in which a husband's inability to be completely honest resulted in a disastrous marriage. The girl had married very young, quickly became pregnant and lost her husband before the baby was born when he left her to resume a long-term homosexual relationship. There are many equally sad cases in which the seeds of disaster were present at the outset, but never revealed until the damage was done.

The need for honesty will be questioned by some people who may believe that there should always be a little mystery in every relationship. Certainly there is nothing more delightful than the voyage of discovery in a new relationship that keeps revealing more surprising aspects of the lady's character. It's a kind of seventh veil that conceals the final revelation and I see no problem with this. I had been married for some time to a woman who surprised me one day by producing a perfect soprano voice from the shower. She had lived for years with the conviction that her voice was ugly and had chosen to conceal it from me to that time. I was able to convince her to have it trained and singing together became a great pleasure for both of us.

Revelations like these can be delightful surprises but others, coming too late in the relationship, can create great obstacles to a happy association. Discussions of lifestyle expectations and revelations about one's feelings should be frank and complete. If it ultimately gets down to the realization that there are too many differences in outlook to allow for compromise then the talking has served its purpose. The compromises though may be more achievable than you believe. A friend of my younger days was a very competitive yachtsman and spent every weekend on the water. It was a problem for his bride-to-be and nearly ended in their abandoning the relationship. She solved the problem by learning to sail and became as dedicated as he. On the other hand a golfer friend gave the game away and played tennis instead, a game at which his wife was also very proficient.

At a deeper level there are also the more serious aspects to the way a couple live together. The question of children is probably the most important of these because starting a family is an irreversible decision and it involves the happiness of other people who have no say in the process. If either partner has children already the decisions for future family blendings become critical in the extreme. Family counseling would seem to me to be almost mandatory in this case, because no one will know just what stresses will be presented with stepparenting until they have experienced them.

It is also important that a couple discussing a future life together should fully understand what expectations the other has for his or her personal fulfillment. Many men I know have been left confused and angry when they discover that their wives are pursuing career paths that take their focus off their husbands and families. It is a phenomenon of our society that women have learned that it is possible to start a new career in midlife when the demands of motherhood are reduced . . . and more power to them. But for a man who has expectations of the little woman tending hearth and home for his comfort there is a rude shock coming! Better check it out now so you can adjust to the change that is going to happen. Even more importantly make sure you really want her to do her own thing. You won't be any help to her if you accept your fate grudgingly and with a sense of martyrdom. You must share her sense of achievement and feel pride in her accomplishments if you are to really be a couple.

Everyone thinks it's important to have enough money, but there is a great gap in the amounts people see as enough. Money values or a dissension about money between partners can be a dreadful bone of contention and leads often to violent argument. Most women I believe have more respect for money than most men do. Women have a greater need for security by and large, and consequently have less gambling instinct. Think about the number of men who have lost their wives as they have lost their fortunes. The recession produced many business failures and many retrenchments . . . along with many breakups. My own wide circle of associates and friends contains an alarming number of examples of this phenomenon. It seems that it is difficult for most women to sustain respect for a husband who is not able to provide for the family. And the other side of this coin is that in cases where the woman has gone to work to bring in the bread, it has created a severe loss of self-esteem on the man's part.

In the first flush of a new love affair it is easy to put all these practical considerations into the too-hard file. The old "she'll be right" philosophy is easy to adopt but you know even as you say it that it is not true. It will only be right if you plan for it to be right and that means a lot of very frank, very clear communication. Keep talking.

PASSION

Thou art my life, my love, my heart.
The very eyes of me:
And hast command of every part
To live and die for thee.
                    ROBERT HERRICK

Passionate love has inspired the poets since the invention of words. But more often than not the great love stories have ended in tragedy and sorrow.

Real life tends to support the theory that it is not possible to experience the soaring heights of a truly passionate love without also knowing the despair and loneliness that are the downside. The Greeks had a word for it—or to be precise, two words. Eros described the passionate form of love and Agape related to the more gentle kind which expressed friendship and trust in a close relationship.

Our Western society has given us a rich literature, and more recently films, which lead us to believe that we should all expect to find our happiness in romantic love. By inference we expect that a great passionate love will lead to a lasting and satisfying relationship.

The truth is that passion is an emotion that is as much a part of suffering as it is of joy. It is not possible to take only the highs without having your share of the lows. And the lows can be all-consuming, destructive and deadly. Too often the passion of love can become the passion of hatred.

This is the point at which anger, jealousy, fear, frustration and despair take over our rational minds and leave us paralyzed. Some men find the experience almost emasculating.

Despite all this, most of us, alone and lonely after separation, will be longing for a new love affair. It is natural to feel that we are only one half of a couple seeking its other half. But this really is only something that our society has conditioned us to believe through the illusion of the romantic ideal. Mills and Boon have made a business of it and even as children we hear stories with a "lived happily ever after" ending. But should we expect this to happen in real life? Are we deluding ourselves if we wait and search for the lady of our dreams, or should we settle for the girl next door (or more likely for us, the divorcée next door) who is a "suitable match" as they used to say.

Passionate love to me is simply another facet of passionate living and to live without passion is to not live fully. So I suppose that for someone who is not a product of a passionate instinct that a calmer kind of relationship will suffice. I think, however, that it helps to define our attitude to a new partner if we can extend the definition of passion beyond the most obvious one of sexual passion. Why not include the term passion to embrace all those areas of our life in which we can seek mutual joy? A passion for baseball or Bach is just as important in a long-term relationship as are the more spectacular passions of the boudoir.

Let us pause before we rush into a new relationship and take stock of the real expectations we have of the other person. If we are driven by sexual passion alone (and I don't suggest this is a bad force by any means) should we not also consider the other criteria we would want to apply? I believe there are many criteria we should consider if we hope for a relatively permanent bonding with another person. These criteria will be different for everyone of course, but some of the basic considerations must revolve around these:

    Defined shared objectives
    An agreement on life-style
    Complete trust and respect
    Shared enjoyment of sex.

Some people will tell you that it is important to have shared interests but I don't believe it is that important. Similarly many will point to age differences or cultural differences as a problem in a relationship. I don't think one can generalize about this and indeed my own experience suggests that given a wider agreement on basic criteria, these differences can sometimes be very positive ingredients.

However, all these things are very personal and the one golden rule in establishing a new relationship must be to avoid elements which could be the focus for future conflict. Sex is probably the worst offender in this regard and I would suggest to anyone who goes into a new relationship where there is a problem about sex, that it is asking for trouble at the outset. It is surprising how often you hear of marriages that last only a few weeks and which are abandoned because one of the partners is confronted by unacceptable sexual practices or a reluctance to engage in sex at all in some cases. I know two couples at least who claim they have not had any sex together for many years. We are often optimistic enough to believe that we will educate our partner to a higher degree of enjoyment of sex, but the literature suggests that it is as likely that time will only exacerbate the difficulties.

PARENTING

◆◆◆◆◆◆◆◆◆◆◆◆◆◆◆

*Children's voices wild with pain
Surely she will come again!*
MATTHEW ARNOLD

A phenomenon of the eighties and nineties has been the growing number of men who have adopted the role of sole parent.

John Wilson is a graduate social worker and a single parent of two children. He has written a book called *Single Fathers—Australian Men Take on a New Role*. I commend it to any man who is or may be a single father. It is written from a very personal perspective and discusses details of studies with over eighty single fathers.

The most important things that emerged from the book for me were firstly the satisfying sense of reward that many men seem to acquire in fulfilling the sole-parent role. On the other side of the coin there is much frustration evident from what seems to be undeniable discrimination against male parents. Many feel that the courts and welfare agencies are very biased in favor of women as potentially better sole parents.

In a way this is hardly surprising given that generations of people in Western society have accepted without question the traditional roles of nurturing mothers and breadwinning fathers.

I have referred to the single-father syndrome as a phenomenon of the last couple of decades and it's pertinent to ask why this has occurred. There are several reasons but I think they were summed up by Hugh Mackay when he spoke of a "Pioneer Society" in a 1993 speech. He said, "We have redefined gender roles in the wake of the women's movements. The phenomenon of the 'working mother' is the most potent symbol of this revolution, with almost two-thirds of mothers of dependent children now having either full-time or part-time work outside the home."

While there is said to be a bias in favor of mothers, there is a changing view on the part of courts which used to tend to automatically award custody to mothers. Given the changing social attitudes and the legal and welfare aspects, it becomes apparent that many men will opt for the parenting role. I am aware of several cases where this has been influenced by the father's unemployment and the fact that the employed mother was able to pay some maintenance to the father who received single-parent allowances. This is role reversal indeed and for some men it could be a psychologically dangerous situation. But from my reading it seems that many men are happy to adopt the parenting role and often derive satisfaction in the bonding they experience with their children.

In a way they are to be envied because I think one of the negative aspects of our society is the lack of time for children that is available to the average male breadwinner in a conventional work environment. My own experience as a single father was not typical of today's single parenting. In the first place I was able to employ a full-time live-in housekeeper. This in itself created as many problems as it solved, with my concerns about her caring for three small children a continual nagging worry. My memories of that difficult period are of constant compromise between the demands of a management job, the need and desire to spend time with my kids, and the maintenance of some kind of social life of my own. There were compelling reasons to think about marriage as a way of bringing my family life back to some kind of proper order.

Marriage after a couple of years of this abnormal lifestyle did in fact solve some of the problems. I had become friendly with a colleague who was attractive, capable and a wonderful hostess and home manager. She ran a tight ship and was a huge asset in my business which had a major entertainment component. Sadly I was not wise enough to realize what a huge task I had asked her to undertake. I wish I had known as much about stepparenting then as I do now.

In hindsight I believe I would have been wiser to opt for taking more of the parenting role on my own shoulders. It's easy to be wise after the event, but I believe I could have resigned my job and worked as a free lance at home, as I had done before. With some domestic help it would have been possible to maintain an income and to supervize the children's care at a closer range. This backward glance is not by way of regret, but it is useful to find some wisdom in the past. What I am saying is that a man who can adopt the sole-parent role is likely to have much reward, not only now but in the future.

For those men who are trying to maintain the twin roles of carer as well as parent, the challenge is great. One man I know has been in this situation for several years already and admits to being continually tired. He has little social contact and is biting the bullet until the kids are old enough to give him more freedom. But he is in no doubt as to the wisdom of his course and really does enjoy his children's company. It is also quite clear that he does not intend to share the parenting task with anyone. "Another couple of years down the track I'll be able to think about a relationship when the kids don't need me," he told me.

Single fathers have another problem as a rule which can add to the stress associated with child-caring. That is the question of involvement by the other parent, either in terms of access or a shared caring role. I have too often witnessed the mental cruelty that angry parents can inflict on each other and the emotional blackmail that sometimes occurs. The effect on children can be traumatic and can also lead to the children becoming very manipulative of both parents as they recognize how vulnerable they have become. Several times I have heard parents of both sexes assert that access visits affected their children so dramatically that it took a week for them to settle down again. Just as they get back to normal it's time for the next visit. One couple I know agreed to longer but less frequent visits to overcome this problem.

With all the tremendous problems that go along with the acceptance of the role, the father who takes it on with courage, love and conviction, is, I believe, likely to derive big rewards in time. Our children are with us for such a brief time, as one realizes after they have grown up. I envy those parents who are able to make the full contribution to their children's growth. The bonds are wonderfully strong if we develop them young, and they last a lifetime.

STEPPARENTING

*Anybody who hates children
and dogs can't be all bad.*
W. C. FIELDS

Of all the complications for a marriage or any other close relationship, the most difficult must be stepparenting. As all parents know, children, if not the hostages of fortune as they used to be described, are certainly the harbingers of conflict—and that's even the case in a regular nuclear family where both parents have blood ties.

When one of the parents is replaced by a stepparent it can be a matter of bitter resentment, though this of course is not always the case. Children's loyalties and affections seem to have a persistence that tends to confirm the old adage that blood is thicker than water. Fathers in particular seem to be able to commit all kinds of role failures and yet manage to survive with their children's affections intact. So when another man comes in to replace him, the newcomer generally has a big task ahead of him in simply getting acceptance. And in many cases the situation is made worse by competition for the mother's affection and attention.

A family I knew had a violent alcoholic father who had injured his wife repeatedly, had verbally abused the children and then brought the marriage to a dramatic end by simply not coming home after a binge. Even though the children had suffered from his anger, they soon began to ask where Daddy was and even blamed their mother for his absence. When she later developed a relationship with a man who wanted to move into the home and take care of them, the children effectively killed the idea with their open and aggressive hostility. Although they were old enough to understand that their father's return would have meant more abuse, they still resisted the idea of another man replacing him.

Even when such open aggression is not evident, children can be very manipulative. Even the nicest children can sense from an early age the opportunity to take advantage of the new dynamics provided by the arrival of a willing victim, as the new stepfather is likely to be.

Little girls in particular are capable of the most outrageous manipulation and will sometimes cultivate the affection of a stepfather with blatant feminine wiles. And most men love it! One friend had his marriage quite seriously threatened by his stepdaughter's attentions which created a significant level of jealousy on the mother's part. They were wise enough to seek counseling and peace was restored long enough for the daughter to form a teen-age attachment to a young man whom she subsequently married.

If this all sounds a bit alarming for a prospective stepfather, let me say I also know many cases where stepfathers have been very successful and have been able to adapt to the new role and bring a depth of affection and stability to the whole family. I have a friend who was glad to be out of a difficult second marriage to a domineering woman but who is acutely missing his stepchildren.

There can be great depth in the bonding between stepfathers and stepchildren and the bonds often last through a lifetime. I know several women who treasure their relationships with stepfathers and there are also men who will tell you that their stepfathers were "good buddies." Whether the roles have been deliberately set to duplicate the parent role or not is probably not important as long as there is a genuine respect and affection involved. The nature of the role in fact will probably be dictated to some extent by the ages of the children. Young children will naturally adopt a stepparent as a full parent more readily than older ones. Often it is possible for older children to accept a stepfather more readily when he is cast in the role of a kind of older brother. This can limit the need for parental disciplines and may be a valuable adjunct to maintaining the peace.

The maternal instinct is a powerful one and every stepfather should recognize it as a potentially dangerous ingredient in a marriage. For most women it is a reflex action, often triggered by relatively minor incidents. It is rarely rational yet it can cause huge rifts in the family. Parent and stepparent need to be very understanding of the pressures that children can exert on a relationship, often without knowing what they are doing.

The golden rule is to never exhibit factional attitudes in front of the children. Wise parents will bite their tongues when a confrontation is happening and keep their judgment for a private discussion when they are alone. When children of any age see that there is disagreement between parents they will have to be saints to not take advantage of the situation and exploit it for their own ends.

Stepsons, stepdaughters, young, old, whatever the permutations and combinations, the formula is never the same and is always unpredictable. The only thing that is predictable is that stepparenting will be a challenge. Every child is an enigma in his/her own right and every grouping of people in a family will have its own peculiar dynamics. There are many good counseling services designed to help you understand these new roles and they could save you much unhappiness in the future. Much understanding and compassion will be needed if it is going to work and a very clear definition of the rules is mandatory. It will clearly be one of the subjects that will need to be spelled out when you get to write that Contract.

CARETAKING

*One fool at least
in every married couple.*
HENRY FIELDING

Charles and Joy have been married for over thirty years and I have known them for most of that time. I always thought of them as very loving people with a successful family and a good circle of friends. They are fun to be with and I have never heard either of them say anything unkind to the other.

I discovered only recently that Charles is an alcoholic and has been for many years. Joy has protected him from the world for all that time and has become an expert at denial, as indeed have the children. Charles is alcohol-dependent and Joy is what psychologists call a co-dependent. Sometimes people like Joy are referred to as enablers, and in fact their chosen role is to support a partner in a way that "enables" him or her to continue with the dependency or addiction. Joy is a natural caretaker and the world is full of people like her.

Caretakers are themselves the subject of psychological definition and it seems that they learn their skill at an early age in the family environment. They are people who as a rule derive their own self-esteem from the feeling of being needed by another person.

It is not only alcoholics who attract caretakers. Hypochondriacs frequently end up with caretaker partners who spend their lives propping up their affliction by removing the need to be active. Drug addicts and people with eating disorders, gambling habits or any other addiction will often find their co-dependent who willingly supplies the missing strength. In a way both parties to dependency/co-dependency are addicts.

It seems that caretakers are instinctively attracted to people who need their kind of dedicated support. When they lose one partner, caretakers generally end up with another partner who is dependent. I met one woman who has been married three times, each time to an alcoholic man. She was also the child of an alcoholic father. It's apparently a common pattern for co-dependents.

Caretaking is unrewarding for all concerned. It's unrewarding for the caretakers because it prevents them from achieving fulfillment in their own lives. Their focus is often so directed at their dependent partner that they have little strength for themselves or anyone else. It's equally unrewarding for the dependent persons because they are being denied the opportunity to assert their own independence. The tragic thing is that the caretaker not only fails in the long run to materially help the addict, but in fact compounds the problem through the enabling process. The alcoholic who is protected from the full effects of his addiction will never be able to achieve recovery as long as a screen of denial and pretense is built around him by his caretaker.

The final tragedy of the caretaker's dedication to this lost cause is that it will ultimately produce a sense of hostility and resentment on the part of the dependent which can result in violence or at best a parting of the ways. Typical of this scenario is the story of Richard who has been an alcoholic since he was twenty. Despite his addiction he became a successful academic mainly through the support of a loyal wife who put up a good pretense that the family was a normal happy one.

After twenty years of tenuous marriage Richard left home without warning or explanation and took up an overseas appointment. His wife was shocked and deeply distressed that he could abandon her and the children and feels she has been grossly betrayed. She feels angry that after her years of loyalty he could simply dump them. He on the other hand describes his action as an escape "from the shackles of dependency." Her dedicated caretaking has done nothing to save him and it has left her with her life in tatters and children who may well be affected for life.

One of them in fact is already showing signs of becoming a teenage alcoholic.

When you are contemplating a new relationship it is wise to analyze what role you are likely to be cast for. Think also about the roles you have already played and ask yourself if you want to do that again. And ask yourself too whether you have a tendency to adopt the same patterns. If you've been a caretaker in the past do you want to play this game again? Or do you feel comfortable about being smothered by a caretaker who sees you as her responsibility for the future?

You may choose to go into a relationship where either of these possibilities exists but you need to clearly understand what to expect. Your emotional integrity could be at stake if you don't recognize the signs of a dependency/co-dependency relationship. It may take a long time to discover what you have taken on and it's generally very hard to change the pattern once it's been established.

Caretaking is of course very different to caring. Caring in the best relationships is a mutual thing and is only positive. Caretaking, however, is largely one-sided and implies giving on the one hand and taking on the other. Caring in the best relationships seems to be something which is tacitly understood between the partners and emerges spontaneously when it is needed. Either partner is capable of giving and receiving the caring act when it is needed.

I asked one couple whom I regard as almost the perfect couple how they reconcile the fact that they are both very strong independent characters. She told me: "When Brian is down I have to be up. When I am down he is wonderful." That to me is what caring is about and it has nothing to do with caretaking.

I believe when we seek a new relationship that we should avoid falling into the role of caretaker. Even if it makes you feel important, it will ultimately stifle your partner's growth and of course your own. Equally importantly, don't allow someone else to become your caretaker. We are all here to fulfill our own destinies and no one can do it for us.

LIFE-STYLES

Many people when they fall in love
Look for a little haven from the world.
BERTRAND RUSSELL

Most of the people I know with apparently stable relationships seem to enjoy the same kind of life-style. Simple things like enjoying the same kind of music are important unless you can live somewhat isolated lives. There is no more disturbing sound to me than the high-decibel mix of hard rock and the Berlin Philharmonic playing the *Eroica*. This can be an exquisitely painful experience which epitomizes the tension that destroys a relationship. If musical tastes are totally disparate perhaps they can be compromised with the adoption of headsets, but all in all two people with similar tastes in music will gain much joy from the sharing of a favorite symphony or an evening of jazz in a basement.

The requirement to endure any unpleasant experience for the sake of one's partner is likely to cause long-term resentment and finally lead to friction. And hours spent listening to the wrong kind of music can be excruciating. By the same token we need to remember that some things are an acquired taste and we should keep an open mind about learning new appreciations.

My first wife was passionately devoted to ballet and one of our extravagances was regular attendance at every new performance that came to town. Initially my involvement was motivated by a desire to be agreeable, but I soon found myself hooked. In due course we got to know many dancers and learned to judge their styles much as some people might follow the careers of favorite football stars. I was soon able to speak with authority about the wonderful elevation of some new prima ballerina or the quality of another's *entrechat*. Ballet became for me a real source of enjoyment and to an extent the cause of some amusement for male friends who saw it as a strictly female form of entertainment in that era.

Adopting new interests can be rewarding and very bonding. On the other hand you may find that there are some areas about which you and a future partner will need to agree to disagree. A simple habit may be unacceptable to one or the other partner and that can be a real problem. Have you noticed how often in the lonely hearts advertisements you read the request for only non-smokers to reply? This can be a real hassle particularly for those who have been unable to give up the habit themselves. One couple I know have overcome his inability to give up cigarettes by agreeing that there shall be no smoking in the house. His periodic visits to the porch are tenable in the summer but he sometimes cheats by retiring to the bathroom in the winter.

I mentioned earlier that in the search for diversion it is good to find some form of activity which will be not only a distraction but also a source of possible meetings with compatible people. To some extent, by being involved in something you enjoy you are more likely to meet other people who will share your interests. The opportunities to meet compatible companions are improved although there is no guarantee that all your interests will be similar. Nevertheless, it is often the case that people with interests of one kind will have wider-ranging compatibility in many areas of life-style.

Nothing is ever perfect so we should not hope to find the perfect partner next time around. But we may get a little closer by looking in the right places and by being aware that other people's life-styles can be very different to our own. If you meet someone whose life is totally different from yours you may need to do some very hard thinking about the future viability of the relationship. Will you be able to adapt to her life-style expectations? Will she be prepared to change? Can you find an acceptable compromise that will be satisfactory to both of you?

Perhaps more important than the outward manifestations of life-style are the basic human traits that can't be changed. A friend of mine is essentially a dreamer, a bit of a Peter Pan in fact, who is happy to live in a cerebral world of his own. His wife, from whom he is now parted, is a practical, active, assertive woman who would undoubtedly be happier with a man who is an achiever. They were passionately attracted to each other after the end of unhappy marriages. They tumbled into the sack and into the early discovery that his world and hers were miles apart except in bed. She thinks he is lazy, impractical, irresponsible. He thinks she is dictatorial, manipulative, intolerant. Each admits that the other is a wonderful lover. Last heard of they were living separately but periodically sleeping together. He concedes that it's an unsatisfactory life-style and I have no doubt that both will be looking for something better in the future.

When you consider how much of our life is spent in the company of a partner we need to take stock of the quality of that time. If it's going to be predictably boring or distressing, then we should be very, very careful about making a commitment we can't be sure of. We only have one life and if we allow someone else to destroy its quality we will be unhappy ourselves and unquestionably make our partner unhappy too.

REDEFINITIONS

Wild spirit which art moving everywhere
Destroyer and preserver; hear, oh, hear!
PERCY BYSSHE SHELLEY

As you approach the time when you could be entering into a new relationship, it might be wise to stop and reflect that the times they are a-changing. Particularly if you are of an older generation it may be difficult to recognize just how far the women's movement has changed the society in which we live.

The invention of the Pill gave women the power to define their own lives and escape from the tyranny of unwanted pregnancy. The women's movement used this power to build a society that is changed beyond belief in both material and philosophical ways. The change has left many men confused and uncertain about their role in this new order in which dependency on a man is no longer essential.

There has been such a radical redefinition of the gender roles that we need to fully understand how they will affect us in a new relationship. But first we need to understand just what has happened to our society.

The first major factor is that women have moved firmly into the workforce. The last couple of decades have seen the emergence of the "working mother" phenomenon. Added to this is the fact that more women are electing to marry at an older age than did their mothers, and significant numbers are deciding to have children outside marriage. There is a dramatic rise in the number of single parents and a significant number of these are men.

All in all it's a gloomy outlook for a man who wants to cling to the old concept of "Me Tarzan, you Jane." Certainly there are still some women out there who will subscribe to the notion that the gender roles are unchanged. In fact it surprises me just how many women I meet who seem very happy with the traditional roles of wife and mother. If that kind of woman interests you as a life partner you may be lucky enough to find her. On the other hand there is much to be said for sharing life with a woman who has her own set of criteria and her own agenda. If you can share with her not only the importance of the career paths of each but also the day-to-day business of running a house and family, then I think there will be great rewards for both of you.

Unfortunately for too many men a wife's ambitions become a threat and can leave them resentful and even angry. The old male/female stereotypes are hard to eradicate.

This is not to suggest that we should all rush into immediate arrangements for role reversal, although many men find this acceptable. The more common situation in contemporary relationships seems to be sharing of roles. Even where the man is working and the woman is at home, there is generally a feeling that both should share the domestic tasks. I have friends who are arguing about the equitability of this arrangement and it seems very likely that they will separate soon because he feels that he is being unfairly imposed upon. It is this kind of thing I had in mind when I referred earlier to the need to get the ground rules straight in the first instance before the relationship is formalized.

I think it is unfortunate that this growing independence on the part of women should leave men so disturbed. We should really be grateful that it is now possible to have a partner who is able and willing to share the load in all our areas of endeavor. I was always conscious in my early years as a young father and breadwinner of the awful responsibility I seemed to have in my accepted role. There was never any question about rights or wrongs—simply it was a fact that "men must work and women must weep, for there's little to earn and many to keep" as the old rhyme had it.

I envy and admire those young families in which both partners work on an equal footing to produce income and at the same time share the parenting roles. And even more I marvel at the men who happily adopt a role reversal to allow their partners to follow their career ambitions. I know one couple who have already exchanged roles twice, with the husband currently working from home so his wife can complete a university degree.

In today's society everything is possible. But nothing except unhappiness will result from going into a relationship in which either party is not satisfied with the role definitions. Our culture places much importance on the labels by which we like to be known. "Housewife," "Manager," "Teacher" are all acceptable in their right context. But such labels as "Househusband" can cause a negative feeling in some people. In any new relationship we must be quite sure that our own and our partner's self-esteem is not going to be impaired by getting tagged with an unacceptable label.

CONTRACTS

*A verbal contract isn't worth
the paper it's written on.*
SAM GOLDWYN

We learn to understand the principle of contracts at an early age even though we don't realize what they are. "If you're a good boy I'll buy you an ice cream" is the kind of contract our mothers introduced us to as little boys. As we grew up contracts became more important and more complex and began to dominate our working lives and to intrude upon our personal lives too.

Of all the contracts we have to live by, probably the marriage contract is the most important one for most of us. Yet today for many people the marriage vows are seen as little more than a symbolic rite with little relevance to real life. In any case marriage is not the only kind of relationship you may be considering. But whatever kind of relationship you go into it is important that you have a clear understanding mutually of what is expected from each partner. In other words a contract.

Some people may feel that the implications of a contract are inhibiting and deny the individual personal freedom. I believe this is not true and that freedom for the individual is in fact enhanced by the adoption of a contract, simply because there is an understanding at the outset of what constitutes freedom. The contract is there to protect the respect and trust that both partners are entitled to expect, and it should not be seen as restrictive.

Contracts will vary from couple to couple in major degrees according to the nature of the relationship and the expectations they have of each other. Sometimes it is a good idea to start with a short-term provisional contract which can be reviewed from time to time as the partners grow and become more attuned to each other's needs and wants. People's ideas have a habit of changing as marriage goes through its growth phases. For others a more permanently defined contract may be desirable. This takes us back to the kind of contract the churches espouse, with clearcut rules that go all the way "till death us do part." Discussing this question of contracts with many people as I have been working on this book, I have been surprised at how many see value in the old rules. Surprisingly this view is held by many younger people who have not yet married.

One shouldn't be surprised at this because history has a habit of presenting society with cyclic patterns. The kids who grew up in the permissive society of the 1960s and 1970s seem to have returned to a set of values much more like their grandparents' than their parents'.

Whether you base your contract on Christian values or make it a more liberal agreement, I think it needs to be written down and formally agreed. Mr Goldwyn is right in suggesting that a verbal agreement is not enough. It's too easy later on to dispute facts or meanings which were agreed verbally some time before. The worst kind of relationship breakdowns seem to happen when one partner does or says something which is unexpected and unacceptable to the other. So contracts need to look at all the aspects of a close relationship.

Infidelity is probably one of the most persistent causes of breakdown. A contract may not eliminate the emotional pulls that lead to infidelity but at least the understanding is there in the contract of what is expected. Many couples fail to address this issue at the outset and discover too late that their ideas are different. For one partner a flirtation may be very hurtful, while for another the occasional sexual dalliance may be acceptable.

There are shades of meaning in these definitions and they need to be part of the contract, or if you prefer to adopt a current term, a letter of intent. In fact this is not a bad way to begin, because intent is what it is all about. Our first need is to state what the intentions of each party are; departures in the future from this intent can then be evaluated and possibly redressed.

Fidelity, important as it is to most relationships, is by no means the only condition that needs spelling out. For some people apparently minor things can have significant effects on the maintenance of a peaceful relationship. Questions of personal hygiene for example are very important to many people. Once while I was conducting a focus group researching a client's product, one of the women on the panel asserted that she never allowed her husband to come to bed until he had showered and cleaned his teeth. It raised a chuckle in the group, but another woman, clearly envious of this, said, "My old man won't even take his socks off." It really amounted to the fact that one woman was happy with the contract she had with her husband; the other was unhappy because she clearly had no contract.

Punctuality, drinking habits, smoking, drugs, social activity, manners and almost every facet of human behavior can be the subject of disagreement. Things that at the beginning of a relationship are mildly irritating can become intolerable as the first flush of romance fades. Most of these things are too trivial to be an issue and in most cases there can be a trade-off. He says, "OK, I'll remember to put the toilet seat down if you stop squeezing the toothpaste from the middle." She says, "I'll let my hair grow if you shave your moustache off."

Contracts are essential when you are sharing a home. Rules about money and budgets, sharing of domestic tasks and the minutiae of daily living need to be spelt out explicitly. It is surprising how many people go into a relationship without any understanding of what is expected. A friend went into his second marriage to discover that his new wife literally could not cook. His first wife had been a magnificent cordon bleu chef who never allowed him in the kitchen except to wash up. He naturally assumed that all women were great cooks. They solved the problem by attending cooking classes together—at which, incidentally, he excelled.

Whether we like it or not, every relationship is in itself an implicit contract. The important thing is that this contract should be defined and understood by both parties so that future arguments don't start with the classic opener "But I thought we agreed that . . ." To be successful the rules need to be discussed and preferably written down. This is not to suggest that they should be inflexible. In fact there could be something that says in effect "We agree that this contract should be reviewed periodically to ensure that it remains consistent with our growing, changing needs and aspirations."

With an established contract with which both parties are happy, there is at least the foundation for a lasting relationship. It is by no means a guarantee but at least it removes the major danger of misunderstanding. Add to this a continuing honest level of communication and we can be confident that the future is as well prepared as we can hope.

RELIGIONS

*The true meaning of religion is thus
not simply morality, but morality touched by emotion.*
MATTHEW ARNOLD

The nexus between relationships and religions is an ancient one and despite the declining influence of the churches, at least in Western society, there is still a strong belief that marriage is part of the fabric of a religious-based society. Saturday afternoons are still the time for white ribbons on stretch limos, and the time-honored service in a church with a minister or priest in robes that are his hereditary badge of office.

Many of the bridal couples will probably not visit their church again until they return for the firstborn child to be christened. I know many couples who have never been inside a church except to attend weddings or funerals. So it is hard to understand why it is so important for people who are not religious to adopt the traditional church wedding. The only explanation that seems to make sense is that people need a ritual to mark this important event in their lives. And of course the churches have all respected the power of ritual and used it as a part of the strength of their social appeal. There is an element of theater in some services and those particularly in Catholic cathedrals and the Great Synagogues can be awesomely moving.

But when the last strains of the wedding march have faded into silence the cynic may be forgiven for asking whether the ritual has significantly altered the prognosis for the durability of the union. The old precepts of the Rabbinical teachings have little relevance today and may even be seen as archaic by some people. "Forsaking all others," "In sickness and in health," "Till death us do part," are the remnants of Judaic law that many will now see as irrelevant in the Western world in the last part of the twentieth century. On the other hand our society has not provided any alternative guidelines for people going into marriage, and the changes have left many people in doubt as to what they should be basing their marriage or their relationships in general on, by way of acceptable rules.

Whether or not you subscribe to the religious conviction that provides a belief in these church precepts, I think it is foolish to throw out the directions until we have another map to guide us through the matrimonial maze. The need to write our own rules is dealt with in the chapter on contracts, and in writing our guidelines down perhaps the best starting point is with the biblical ones. Modify them perhaps, but bear in mind they have served society for a long time, and pause before you throw the rope after the bucket.

In the past, religious prejudice was in itself a hazard in marriage. My parents with their Protestant lineage would mutter darkly about "mixed marriages" and I used to think that there was some fiendish fate in store for me if I should fall for a Catholic girl. There was a family story about a distant relative who had married a high-cast and very wealthy man from India. When told about the marriage my Gran asked if he was "very black." Yes, she was told, he is a very dark gentleman. "But not Catholic I hope?" she said. It is hard to realize that only fifty years ago such prejudices existed and that they had such dramatic and often disastrous effects on relationships. Society has made some progress, thank goodness, and little significance is attached today to mixed religions in marriage.

A last remnant of the churches' influence on marriage seems to be in the counseling area, and many of the churches have very fine counseling services. Yet even these seem to be diminishing in importance as more academically trained people move into the field. The role of the minister in guiding his parish in this area has become relatively less important and in some cases I think this may be a good thing.

I was once referred to a Protestant minister for counseling. After listening to me for a while he said, "Look, I've been married to the same lady for the past forty years. I've never slept with another woman. I can't even begin to understand what you're talking about." For a moment I almost envied his ordered existence.

For those who enjoy the support of a church community there is undoubtedly a lot of comfort to be derived from the group dynamics, aside from the spiritual faith. When a couple share this faith it can be a powerful force for good in a marriage. But when one partner is pressuring the other to conform, then that in itself can be a problem that may need to be examined. Like every other element in a relationship, communication about this disparity of beliefs is essential.

MONOGAMY

If you are afraid of loneliness, don't marry.
ANTON CHEKHOV

In our society the concept of monogamy is still seen as the norm. In practice it is probable that the idea of enduring monogamous relationships may be regarded as a matter of personal choice. Many people subscribe to what a (lady) friend of mine describes as "serial monogamy," that is the belief that it is appropriate to change relationships provided that each is separate from the others. It is unusual today to meet many people who have remained permanently in one relationship to the exclusion of others.

Needless to say there are many marriages in which lip service is paid to the concept of monogamy but in which extramarital relationships have occurred. Sometimes these are acknowledged, even condoned. In other cases they are clandestine. Fidelity in marriage is not unfortunately universal and there are many people who will say that this is normal and acceptable.

Essentially there seem to be these options when you set the rules for a permanent relationship:

Permanent monogamy ("forsaking all others")
Serial monogamy (one to one until we change partners)
Open "marriage" (either partner allowed others)
Covert infidelity (pretend monogamy).

In looking at these options, as we should do when we enter a relationship, two important things need to be considered. The first is that whatever option is adopted, it should be with the complete agreement of both parties. A reluctant acquiescence won't work in the longer term, even if it seems OK to start with. Sooner or later the reluctant acquiescer will begin to resent the feeling of having the worse end of the bargain and resentment will lead to anger. This particularly applies where sexual codes are in dispute. I have known several people who profess to enjoying a so-called "open marriage"—on examination though, one or the other partner is found to be unhappy with the other's "infidelity," as it is judged to be.

The second important consideration is to make sure that whatever rules the game is played by, these do not in any way disturb the fulness of the couple's commitment to each other. Commitment is of course a very personal matter and is different for everyone. Here again it is essential that the nature of the commitment is agreeable to both parties and is not in any way compromised by the actions of either person.

One very loving couple I knew well had a tacit understanding that he was likely to have the odd affair, particularly when he was traveling, which he did a good deal. Everything was fine as long as he was discreet and did not embarrass his wife. Disaster struck when one of his passing fancies decided to stake a claim on his emotions and confronted the wife. It was a very testing time but I am happy to say that the marriage survived after some solid soul-searching. There was a good deal of pain all round and one probably has to feel some sympathy for "the other woman" who might be seen as the victim of this eternal triangle.

Steve Biddulph in *The Making of Love*, speaking of monogamy, says: "Because of the trust involved in allowing such deep access to your being, it is not possible to be involved sexually with more than one partner and expect anything but confusion . . . Adultery is a sure path to pain." The truth of this statement is, I believe, central to the whole question of making a relationship work. Without commitment and without trust there cannot be a real relationship. And as sure as hell there is no way trust and commitment can survive where there is infidelity. I use the word in its broadest sense of meaning disloyalty. Infidelity doesn't have to be sexual and can be just as destructive if it is nothing more than a repetition of the famous cliché "my wife doesn't understand me." The probability is of course that she does understand you very well, you louse!

The great lovers of history from Don Juan to Errol Flynn have always seemed to be enviable creatures to some men who have trod the righteous path of conformity. But think about the misery that most of them have seen despite the multiple relationships. Most have ended up lonely and unloved and as often as not, with painful and destructive social diseases to bring their lives to a sorry end.

Monogamy it seems is the go if you really want to be happy. Mentally and physically it is the healthy way. I read pamphlets from time to time about "safe sex" and one I saw today in my doctor's waiting room had rather unpleasant diagrams showing the use of condoms which were recommended when the casual partner's "HIV status was unknown." Wow! I am about to copulate with a person who might have AIDS, so I put my trust in a flimsy latex product which will all but reduce the act to a cerebral experiment in imitation lovemaking. Thanks, but no thanks!

Think in contrast about the sheer joy of knowing that you and your partner are so committed that the question will not come up about AIDS, gonorrhea, syphilis, herpes, etc. etc. etc. Trust is a wonderful ingredient for producing great happiness in a loving relationship. And without monogamy I believe trust is not possible.

If this all sounds judgmental let me say that it is simply one philosophy. Other viewpoints will recognize a more open and permissive pattern of sexual behavior when both partners agree to the rules. For some people sexual infidelity will be of much less importance than other issues in the relationship. Essentially each couple will have to decide what is and is not important.

Having said this one then has to ask if permanent monogamy is a practical concept. A monogamously based relationship is possible at any time, at any age, as long as you want it and need it. And that leads me to speculate on whether or not monogamy is essentially a serial thing if you want it that way. Is there in fact a season for our loving relationships? Is it possible that we were not intended to adopt the "Till death us do part" philosophy?

Should we be happy to accept that the beauty of a genuine love is as transient as that of the rose which fades inevitably with time? Is there truth in the old folk song that says "Love when it's old, it groweth cold/ and fades away like the morning dew"?

I believe that for people with sensitivity and integrity there is the possibility of deep and intense relationships happening at any time in their lives. There are times after a parting when you will feel that this is a hopeless pipe dream. Reckless one-night stands or compromise affairs may seem the answer. My fervent hope is that you will come again to realize the true worth of another monogamous, trusting commitment. Perhaps we were never intended to be permanently monogamous in the first place. Maybe we were meant to be serially monogamous partners. Think about it before you give up and become a Don Juan or worse, a recluse.

DIVORCE

When married people don't get on they can separate, but if they're not married it's impossible. It's a tie that only death can sever.

W. SOMERSET MAUGHAM

Sometimes a separation may seem final right up to the point of filing for divorce. Then the finality of the act makes itself apparent and often people about to divorce will take a deep breath and reconsider the future. This is the time to really ask yourselves some searching questions and decide if you are capable of living without each other for good. A friend of mine actually withdrew his application from the court after a brief reconciliation with his wife, but later resubmitted it when it was evident that the marriage was indeed over.

However, if you have come to an irrevocable decision about divorce, it is best to get on with the process and dispose of the stress it will cause as quickly as you can. Court officials are very helpful in my experience and will guide you through the procedures if you request their help. Many people today are handling their divorces without the help of lawyers and this can be perfectly satisfactory as long as there is no major disagreement about property, custody and maintenance, the areas of most common dispute.

Where there is agreement about the main issues you are probably better off without lawyers, who sometimes tend to aggravate disputes by the very nature of their professional responsibility. How many times have you heard people say that they were reasonably amicable until the lawyers moved in? This is not a criticism of the law or its processes. It is simply a fact that involvement of the law is bound to produce adversarial conflicts.

The courts are aware that this is a period of great stress for most people and provide a counseling service to help couples reach sensible decisions, particularly where the welfare of children is concerned. In fact they give high priority to the ultimate best interests of children in all their deliberations. It is comforting to know that the majority of people going to court have been able to resolve their differences and are able to avoid the cost and distress of courtroom battles and judicial directives.

Naturally counseling is most effective if both partners attend, but if one refuses then the other will still get benefit from the counseling sessions. These are designed to improve communication between the couple and to help them come to grips with the emotional problems they are facing during this difficult period. Hopefully this will help couples to reach agreement, but if there are areas of conflict it may be necessary to get legal advice. The courts will tell you where to begin and indicate what free services are available if you can't afford legal fees.

The whole process of divorce holds a lot of uncertainty for most people, but with sympathetic people to help you at the courts you will find that much of the fear is diminished. No one will deny that it is an unpleasant task to have to formally bring a marriage to an end; but the process is relatively simple and straightforward.

When you consider the importance we place on the ritual of marriage it is strange that there is so little emphasis on the termination of such a profound institution. Suddenly after all those years you are left with nothing but a piece of government paper.

CUSTODY

◆◆◆◆◆◆◆◆◆◆◆◆◆◆◆◆◆

*To lose one parent may be regarded as a misfortune;
to lose both looks like carelessness.*

OSCAR WILDE

When a divorce has been acrimonious the children often suffer from exposure to unresolved conflict between the parents. This is of course greatly to be avoided and most parents will attempt to reach amicable agreement on the questions that directly affect the children. In this case the agreement can be registered with the court setting out the mutual decisions concerning guardianship, custody and access. This agreement can then be enforced by the court as though it were a court order.

In coming to the right conclusions for an agreement, it is necessary to know what the terms guardianship, custody and access mean. I can do no better than quote from a document supplied by the Family Court of Australia:

GUARDIANSHIP involves making decisions about the long-term welfare of the children, that is religion, education, major operations, change of name, etc.

CUSTODY involves making decisions about daily care and control, that is choice of clothing, food, physical care, discipline and other day-to-day issues.

ACCESS is the right of the children to have a continuing relationship with the parent they do not live with. It is best if parents can agree about "reasonable access," that is access which is not strictly defined but which requires that both parents are flexible within the arrangements.

The court is aware that the most appropriate people to make decisions about the children are the parents, and it encourages them to reach agreement on the questions of guardianship, custody and access. The court's counseling service is well experienced to advise parents and in most cases appropriate conditions can be agreed. However, where parents are in dispute over these matters, the court will make a decision. The welfare of the children will be of paramount consideration.

Unfortunately agreement is not always possible and I know a couple of cases in which disagreement between the parents was so violent that the children suffered real trauma in the ensuing battle which was ended with a court order. In one of these cases custody was awarded to the father, and I believe the mother has had no access for some years.

While agreements and court orders are obviously necessary safeguards of children's rights, it is clear that the goodwill of both parents in relation to their children is of prime importance. It will make the effective care of their interests more solid, and will allow the flexibility that changing circumstances may require.

I have a friend who has exchanged custody with her ex-husband at the request of the children, and this seems to have been mutually advantageous to all concerned. It is likely that the children have benefited by the knowledge that both parents care about them sufficiently to want them with them.

It is important that the courts accept the principle of putting the welfare of children at the top of priorities. It should also be the first consideration of caring parents. If you find that disputes about the children are getting out of hand it is important that you seek counseling and if necessary legal advice, before the battle becomes bloody. At all costs the children should be protected from violent dispute.

ACCESS

Do you hear the children weeping, o my brothers
Ere the sorrow comes with years?
ELIZABETH BARRETT BROWNING

Dealing with access to your children can be very painful if you are the non-custodial parent. It will force you into contact with your estranged spouse and it will probably remind the children themselves that they are in the midst of turmoil that tests their divided loyalties. To make access periods work, a lot of understanding and compassion is needed.

Inevitably the custodial parent will have the main tasks of maintaining the realities of life with the children. Homework, discipline and all the mundane, boring things that afflict the child living with a single parent must be doled out by the parent who has elected to take on this role. Forget about popularity. On the other hand the parent with access has the opportunity as a rule to be the fun person that organizes outings and bends over backwards to make the visits a really good time.

Rosemary had custody of her two children and their father never missed a Sunday access visit. He planned the day to make each Sunday memorable for the kids. Amusement parks, the zoo, McDonald's and all kinds of exciting events followed in a program of concentrated entertainment. All they got from Mom was discipline and chores. One night they announced that they wanted to live with Daddy and Rosemary's heart sank. Affecting a nonchalant attitude she helped them pack their bags, and made sure they had all their schoolbooks, dental appointments and musical instruments, promising them that she would remind Daddy to make sure they practised and did their homework. This reminder that life was real and life was earnest produced a long silence and a decision to stay after all.

Access visits sometimes produce very disturbed feelings on the part of children and can be a problem not only for them but for the custodial parent. Several custodial parents have told me that the weekly access visits leave the kids disturbed and fractious for days. One woman said: "They come back on Sundays tired, cranky and obviously unhappy. Their dad has a girlfriend who gives them a bad time. It takes the whole week to get them back to normal and then it's time for the next visit."

Even more disturbing is the situation where a parent doesn't care enough about the children to make their time of access worthwhile. Robert was awarded fortnightly weekend access to his two sons, but after heavy Friday sessions in the bar with his cronies he often forgot which weekend it was, or arrived late to collect the boys. They would sit for hours waiting at the gate for Dad, who was always late, and generally exhibited signs of a bad hangover.

There are many thousands of fathers who have custody of their children, but far more of course who have access rights only. If you are in the latter category and if you are finding it difficult to maintain a relationship with your kids, don't despair. Nothing is constant but change, and you will find as the children grow older their attitudes and behavior patterns will alter. Whatever you do, don't lose touch. Even if letters are the only means of contact, keep them coming.

Take comfort from the fact that children have an infinite capacity for love and loyalty. There will sometimes be outside influences that will make it hard for you to keep your balance, especially as your ex-partner enters into new relationships. With luck such influences may not be all bad and may even help to improve your own position with your children. Hang in there for your kids and don't tolerate any influence that you believe is wrong for them. Remember that the courts are there to protect their interests. Whatever the situation you may have with your ex-partner, the welfare of your children is a sacred trust. You will never regret the time and care you devote to them.

THE LAW

◆◆◆◆◆◆◆◆◆◆◆◆◆◆◆◆◆

The Law is the true embodiment
Of everything that's excellent.
It has no fault or flaw.
And I, my lords, embody the Law.
SIR W. S. GILBERT

Although it is perfectly feasible to process your own divorce without the help of a lawyer, it is sensible to have an understanding of where the law stands on such issues as matters of divorce, the welfare of children of the marriage, dealing with violence and the question of property settlement.

Up until recent times, several grounds were available to divorcing spouses, one of which was adultery. This required evidence of the adulterous behavior of the "guilty" party and resulted in much sordid evidence being required to substantiate an application. Sometimes partners who had agreed to a divorce were obliged to go through the travesty of a manufactured adultery, and there were firms of private investigators who specialized in providing "evidence." This sometimes involved the provision of surrogate lovers, submission of photographs of the couple in *flagrante delicto* and other unpleasant and degrading procedures.

Only one ground is now recognized for divorce and that is the irretrievable breakdown of the marriage. This is seen as related to a separation of the partners for at least twelve months and the assumption that no reconciliation is likely. The courts are not in any way concerned with the allocation of blame and the old issues of adultery, desertion and cruelty are not held to be relevant. The only evidence required is of the separation, plus the assurance that reconciliation is not likely, and finally that the welfare of children of the marriage has been properly considered.

The granting of a divorce means the official termination of

the marriage. However, other matters such as the disposition of property, custody and access to children and questions of maintenance are separate issues which the court deals with if and when disputes arise. Where the couple have reached agreement on these matters it is generally not necessary to get legal advice, but if they are under dispute legal help is necessary.

The best starting point for finding legal help, unless you have a lawyer in whom you have confidence, is probably your local legal aid office. These offices are listed in the Yellow Pages. Some communities also have community legal services. In some circumstances you may qualify for legal aid and if you think you do, you should check this out with the nearest legal aid office. If you decide to employ a lawyer privately, you will be wise to seek a lawyer who is experienced in this field. Your state law society will in most cases give you the names of suitable lawyers.

VIOLENCE AND THE LAW: The process of separation and divorce is often attended by a lot of anger, and it is not surprising that violence sometimes erupts. Although most of the cases reported in the media tend to suggest that men are the main offenders in this regard, this is not a male prerogative by any means and the law is clear in offering equal protection for both men and women against physical violence. Violence committed against a spouse is criminal assault in law and victims of this kind of assault are entitled to bring criminal charges against their spouse. This applies also to violence committed against a child. If you fear that you or your children may be subjected to violence you should immediately contact the police and the courts.

PROPERTY AND THE LAW: Husbands and wives are given equal rights, in principle, to the ownership of property. In many cases the husband is the one to leave the family home, often with minimal possessions. This is generally dictated by the needs of the children and some men fear that in the process they have relinquished their claim to a share of the property. This is not the case. The law takes the view that both partners in a marriage have an equal share in the family home regardless of the financial contributions. The wife is generally seen as having contributed by maintenance of the home and the responsibilities of being a housewife, even if she has made no financial contribution. However, courts do modify this by taking into account the individual incomes of the two spouses and the relative costs involved in supporting children.

It has been said that courts today tend to favor the interests of women, and certainly one hears of some strange anomalies. I know of two cases of men on above-average salaries who are living at almost subsistence levels in small apartments because of the large payments they are making to their ex-spouses. In one case the wife has a live-in de facto residing in the family home and contributing to the income. My friend is understandably bitter at what he feels to be a very unfair disadvantage. I have no way of knowing whether such apparent aberrations occur frequently, but one has to assume that some judgments will defeat the good intentions of the legal system.

It is presumably the result of interpretation that such anomalies will occur, not the structure of the law itself, which seems to be designed for equal rights for both spouses, given the predominant consideration of the children's interests.

A matter which needs to be considered after divorce is the status of wills. These will be affected by your divorce and you should consult a lawyer to ensure that your interests are not in jeopardy.

CHILD SUPPORT AND THE LAW: A close friend spent many years supporting the stepchildren that came with their mother's second marriage while their father consistently evaded every effort to have a court order enforced. Over the years the unpaid maintenance amounted to many thousands of dollars, and my friend's standard of living was significantly reduced in consequence. It seems to be an area in which the law does not always have teeth.

In summary it is clear that by being reasonable, seeking counseling and arriving at mutually acceptable decisions you can limit the need to seek legal intervention. Apart from the costs involved there is generally an attendant increase in the level of aggravation when the law is invoked. If the law does have to be involved you should make sure that you are being well advised by someone who knows the intricacies of this whole area.

PROPERTY

*The price we pay for money
is paid in liberty.*
ROBERT LOUIS STEVENSON

Property issues are often the most contentious of all the arguments confronting a couple when they break up. And often the trivia of life are the most unresolved questions when the old "his-and-hers" squabbles are in full flight.

A couple who have agreed on custody and access issues, have agreed on the disposition of the family home and have arrived at a satisfactory formula for maintenance, may suddenly find themselves in angry conflict over a record, a picture or a piece of furniture. Suddenly all the rational restraints break down as they get locked into a full-scale free-for-all about small items that generally have little material value in the overall scheme.

Why is it that most of us seem to be able to deal with the big issues but fail to maintain our cool when it comes to these small things? I suspect that it is because these small possessions represent very personal symbols of our emotional past, either as a couple during happier times, or in some cases as icons from the life before the relationship started.

A friend with an extensive book collection agreed to have this valued and to have it sold at auction to provide funds for a settlement on his wife. There was one book, however, which he valued specially because it had an inscription to his father from the author and he retained this for himself. When she learned of this his wife became furious and demanded that it be sold separately and the funds divided. His refusal to do this resulted in a breakdown in what had been, if not a cordial relationship, at least something in the nature of an armed neutrality. The actual monetary value was small, and the issue became one of principle.

Another couple I know had major disagreements about a

collection of music tapes which each felt to be of more importance to them than to the other party. They ended up splitting the collection, and it was sad that both had to go about the task of replacing the missing ones by haunting the secondhand stores.

It is important when these minor issues start to endanger a whole relationship that couples be aware of what is happening and do something about it before it escalates into a major disagreement which may ultimately affect bigger issues. Mediation counseling may be the answer if they can't together resolve it amicably and with some dignity. Several groups are dealing with this form of mediation, which is different from marriage counseling. The mediation groups are set up simply to resolve disputes between couples in broken relationships and they do not attempt to mend the relationship. Statistics show that couples in mediation have a very high success rate in reaching agreement on contentious issues.

If a couple is not able to get access to one of the mediation centres, then perhaps a good friend may be able to bring common sense into what may be otherwise a silly but very destructive argument.

MALCOLM'S STORY

Malcolm and Jeanette were married when they were both twenty. She had been a ballet dancer and had shown great promise and a matching ambition. But at sixteen she had fallen victim to anorexia as often happens to dancers, and she became too weak to sustain a performance. Heartbroken at the destruction of her career before it had really begun, she wrestled with the disease.

Recognizing it as the killer she lived with, she forced herself to eat and in the process became bulimic. Bulimia is the condition in which the victim eats well, even overeats in some cases, and then induces vomiting which ultimately becomes involuntary. It's as though the conscious mind is ordering the body to take nourishment, while the subconscious mind is ordering the reverse.

At the time they met, Jeanette was very thin, but seemed in other respects quite healthy and very alert, highly intelligent and a most engaging and attractive companion. She and Malcolm were already very much in love before she told him the full story of her disease and its implications. She had to tell him for example that she had not ovulated for some years and that the prospect of having children was thus remote. She offered to release him from his commitment, but he refused to believe that there was no future for them or that they would not have a normal family, and they were married with the blessing of the church and the two families.

Malcolm was a health fanatic himself and had made dietetics a hobby which he extended to his own considerable skills as an amateur chef. He studied the literature on anorexia/bulimia and began to believe that there was a possibility that much of the cause was chemical, even though the root cause was generally agreed to be psychological. So began a regime which they both followed, in which Malcolm did all the cooking and followed a careful dietary balance of his own design. Jeanette put on weight and had to be constantly reassured that she was not getting grossly fat as she feared.

One night he came home from work and was greeted by a tearful but ecstatic wife. "Darling, I'm having a period!" she said. It was the first she had experienced for nearly five years.

"Nothing I ever do in my life will ever match the triumph of that moment for me," Malcolm says. "I could build a Taj Mahal and feel less sense of achievement than I did at that moment knowing I had brought that woman back to life in the fullest sense." Some time later, Malcolm and Jeanette produced a fine healthy son and a couple of years after that, a daughter.

And that's where we should be able to leave the story with implications of a happily-ever-after ending. Sadly it was not so.

For reasons no one seemed to understand, Jeanette moved away from the dietary regime and began to eat what Malcolm described as "irresponsible" meals. They quarreled about this and as the arguments increased, Jeanette's weight declined until she began to look very emaciated and became weaker and weaker. The declining physical health was accompanied by wild mood swings. Sometimes loving and gentle, she could suddenly erupt into a spiteful angry virago. She would not accept that there was a need for psychological help and began drinking and smoking heavily. Malcolm was helpless and his frustration and despair were immense.

One night he came home to find police at his door to tell him that Jeanette had died in a car accident. She had spun off on a tight mountain bend and had died instantly when the car plunged hundreds of feet into a gorge. The coroner recorded a verdict of accidental death, but Malcolm found a suicide note some time later.

There followed for Malcolm some years of loneliness and a lot of stress bringing his children up as a single father. Although he met many women in the course of his business, he was unable to find a partner and his friendships were nearly all platonic. Sexual frustration was largely sublimated in the unremitting hard work of holding down a job and running a good home for the kids. Once on a camping holiday with the children he had met a lovely woman who, as a single mother, was in much the same situation. They had a brief and passionate affair, but she felt unable to adopt his children as her responsibility and so it became a more and more remote experience, finally petering out altogether. He remained alone right up to the time when the children left home.

Then it happened. Suddenly one day a radiant creature appeared in his office and he knew he was going to marry her. It was a love-at-first-sight meeting for both of them and within weeks they were married. That she had children was of no concern to Malcolm, who in fact almost saw this as a bonus. He soon formed a strong bond with them, particularly the younger one.

Then, bit by bit, it all started to go horribly wrong. Arguments started over trivial matters and got out of hand, turning into major conflicts that sometimes became protracted battles lasting for days on end. The recession came and Malcolm was retrenched. A new focus for tension had entered their already fragile relationship and the comfortable life-style they had enjoyed was abruptly changed to one of some austerity.

The parting was mutually agreed to and Malcolm moved into a small but comfortable apartment. He spent some very unhappy months coming to grips with the fact that he was back in a grief-ridden state of mind which reminded him horribly of his earlier bereavement.

It is two years since the breakup with his second wife and Malcolm is cooking the meal he has invited me to share. He is someone I would describe as a very calm person, but that would not have been appropriate when I first met him. He admits to having had to work hard to arrive at the peaceful state he now enjoys most of the time.

"This place was my escape hatch when I first moved in," he explains. "It was a refuge. Now it is my home and I enjoy being here. I enjoy the *sense of personal space . . . not having to share the solitude. I like being able to come and go at my speed. Selfish? Yes you could say that. But I have learned to treasure the aloneness I have chosen to live with. Aloneness is nothing to do with loneliness. In fact the worst loneliness I can remember was when I was married."*

Malcolm concedes that the possibility of another relationship is not out of the question. "I really am a committed heterosexual," he says, "but it will happen if it's meant to and no one will be more pleased than I. But I am not about to waste time searching for the elusive lady of my future. There are too many important things to do like finish this book that has been on the backburner through two marriages. Sex? Oh, yes of course, I remember how important it was. It would be nice, yes, I suppose so."

He looks out at the distant view, clearly unconvinced that sex is an issue that needs immediate resolution. In his late fifties, Malcolm is fit, energetic and would undoubtedly meet the needs of some lonely lady seeking a "warm, sincere mature gent, non-smoker to share . . . etc." My belief is that such a lady might be lucky to find Malcolm, but on the other hand she would need to have a lot to offer in exchange for his newfound aloneness.

NATHAN'S STORY

Widowed after a happy marriage of twenty-five years, Nathan went into his second marriage with high hopes. Sally was some years younger and a divorcée with two young children. His children were grown up and he felt confident that he could be a good father to the two girls. Left to their own devices they in turn responded to him with great affection and the only sign of trouble was an intermittent streak of jealousy that occasionally manifested itself in Sally when the girls got too close to their stepfather. Nathan and Sally were intelligent enough to recognize the dynamics of the relationship and had discussed the jealousy problem in a very mature way. It was in fact not really a problem at all since they had addressed it.

In due course the older girl left home to live with her fiancé and within a few months the younger one went away to college and boarded with a relative. Nathan and Sally took a well-earned holiday and boasted to their friends about how wonderful their "second honeymoon" had been. Close friends were not surprised by the situation as they had been cited often as the happiest couple in town. They sold their house and bought a run-down farm where they intended to catch up on the things they had never been able to do—in her case painting, and in his the writing of an historical novel he had been researching for some years. Sally was forty and Nathan in his mid-fifties. It seemed that they had found the perfect formula for a happy retirement life surrounded by good friends in a beautiful environment, doing what they wanted to do.

One night Nathan returned from a trip to the city to find Sally's car gone and a note on the stove saying that she had left for good. There was no explanation and no way he could contact her. Phone calls to friends with guarded enquiries made it obvious that Sally had not confided in any of their closer friends. Nathan went out into the garden and vomited, choking back tears and rage and feeling a hopeless despair overtake him.

A day or two later a letter arrived from Sally apologizing for the way she had left without explanation, but confirming that she would not be back and providing a mailbox number for communication. No, she said, there was nothing specially wrong with their marriage. Yes, she conceded his care of them had been as much as she would have expected from anyone. It was simply, she said, that she had to find her own identity, that she was tired of being half of a couple. She needed space for herself.

"My first reaction was a consuming rage. The unfairness of having been dumped after having spent ten years as breadwinner, husband, lover, father and anchorman for the family was devastating," Nathan says. "We had never had an angry word in all ten years together. If she had any problems I never knew what they were—she never told me. We were not well-off but we were comfortable especially since the girls had left. Our sex life was exciting and she often used to tell me I was the only lover who'd ever turned her on properly. It was a nightmare which made no more sense than any other bad dream. I began to realize as the lonely days dragged on that I was making myself ill and I sought counseling to try and help me back to some kind of normality."

Nathan's counseling was a turning point and he wrote to Sally imploring her to also get counseling. She replied angrily that there was nothing wrong with her and that she wasn't going to have shrinks probing into her private life. He soon began to realize that there was no point in seeking a reconciliation. Sally had quickly got into a new relationship as she was eager to tell him in one of her letters, and he wondered futilely whether the man had been on the scene before the breakup. It was academic, because the liaison only lasted a short time and was followed by a whole series of short-term relationships which all seemed to end in unhappy conclusions for Sally.

Eventually Sally contacted Nathan and they met for dinner where she pleaded for a second chance. For some reason he couldn't quite comprehend, she seemed to think the breakup had been mainly his fault and she kept referring to his lack of sensitivity as a cause. He never did discover exactly what she meant by this. However, he did agree to making another attempt to rescue the marriage. She again told him what a wonderful lover he was and how the "others" had disappointed her. Sometimes she would regale him with intimate details of her sexual encounters which he found very distressing. He got to be tired of hearing about Tom with the premature ejaculation problem, Dick with the rough calloused hands, and Harry with the insatiable lusts it seemed of a satyr.

After a few days passionate reunion they parted company with a promise to return together as soon as Sally could dispose of her apartment. Then he had a call from Sally to say she had spent the night with one of her lovers, and that's when he finally started to hate her. He filed for divorce immediately and he says that this act in itself was one from which he derived some kind of strength.

"The next two years were the most miserable I have ever spent in my life," Nathan says. "I would occasionally see the girls but these meetings were awkward for all of us, no doubt because of their divided loyalties. The younger girl was a problem for her mother, having become involved in drugs and drinking, and clearly was disgusted by her mother's behavior since we had split up. I'm sure her behavior was her way of making a statement . . . a protest."

Nathan continued with counseling and moved back to the city where he had friends closer at hand. He joined a debating society, worked hard on his book and made many new friends including several women with whom he formed close but platonic friendships. "These friendships were my salvation," he says. "The women I knew were so much more prepared to listen than most men who seem to be embarrassed to hear anything intimate about someone else's life. I began to realize that I was forming a very close network with people who had similar problems. I called them 'the walking wounded' and we joked about being emotional crocks, and the need for the blind to lead the blind. Eventually several of us realized how important it was to have the trust and understanding of other people and we agreed that we might phone each other at any time. We still do this and for most of us the phone is a lifeline. Only one of my male friends seems to find it strange, and I suspect he finds it all a bit wimpish. He, however, has not been through the mill and I wonder whether he might be more understanding if he should meet with disaster."

Nathan is one of the survivors of the breakup trauma and lives a very complete life. He is still alone four years after the divorce and rarely sees Sally. "I hardly ever think about her now," he says. "There's no anger now and I find it hard to understand how violently I hated her for a while. I really believe I could have killed her at one time. Now I couldn't care less who she's sleeping with or what she's doing with her life. I'm just glad she's out of mine."

Nathan has recently met a woman who he says is "a good friend" and he admits that there is more than the usual stirring of old emotions when they meet. But as he says, there will have to be a lot of compulsion to pass up the freedom of the celibate life.

SILVER LININGS

This morning, the day I set aside to write this epilogue, I unexpectedly ran into a young man whom I had talked to nearly a year ago. Last time I saw him he was living in a scruffy little apartment and was trying to make ends meet by doing ad hoc laboring jobs. He was sole parent to a small daughter and was anxious to spend as much time with her as possible. For that reason he found it difficult to find suitable full-time employment.

I hardly recognized him today as the same man. He was cheerful, confident and clearly in charge of his life. He has started a small business which allows him flexible hours and is thoroughly enjoying the challenge of using his skills as an artisan. He is still in sole charge of his daughter and says she is his greatest "asset." He has come to understand the need for personal space and respects this for his child as for himself. He says they are "great pals." He has a lady friend, he told me, but they have agreed to be close spiritually and emotionally, as he put it, without moving in together.

His evident sense of well-being and self-sufficiency were good to see and I felt a great happiness for him. To me he represents the power that I believe all men possess. Apart from the time we spent talking a year ago, he has had little help from anyone. He admits his friends didn't particularly want to know about his problems, and he felt that he simply didn't have time to get counseling. This lack of time, of course, is an aspect of being alone which is particularly difficult for men who are responsible for children. Many deny themselves the help of counseling either through time constraints or a reluctance to commit their feelings to another person. For whatever reasons, he elected to go it alone, and it seems that he has come through with flying colors.

Today's encounter was one of the happy endings of which I have found many among friends and acquaintances who have survived the dark times to recognize with amazement that there is life after she's left. Not everyone makes it, unhappily, but we should all take heart from the success stories. When the situation seems most dismal, it's good to find someone who has been there and come through again. It can be enormously helpful to hear firsthand stories from survivors at a time when you are just hanging in there hoping you won't perish.

If there is some kind of men's group within your area, it could be worth contacting them to find out what they stand for. Many such groups are starting up all around the world and some, I believe, are very helpful and supportive. I am nevertheless reluctant to recommend any specific ones because what is right for one man could be unacceptable for another. It's something very personal and one needs to advance with caution before making a commitment.

There are also some questionable organizations, I understand, which have set themselves up as pressure groups and are inclined to be extreme in their attitudes to women. Such attitudes are likely to be very destructive and should be avoided, not only because these divisive feelings are dangerous in a societal sense, but also because they are damaging to the individual. Beyond everything we must retain our appreciation of women, no matter how disappointed we may feel about a particular woman.

As I talk to the survivors I marvel at man's capacity not only to survive but to grow and thrive through adversity. It seems that men who have had the courage to face the future without flinching often acquire a strength and resolve that others may never understand. It's almost as though the emotional turmoil that comes with a broken relationship acts as a catalyst to self-realization. Some men of course do not survive and their lives are claimed by death, drink or a rescue-based relationship that does no more than replace the minder.

For men who really survive the trauma, there is an opportunity to rebuild life to a new and better pattern. The process generally starts with a long close look at who we really are and a dispassionate acceptance of the person we see, warts and all. Most of us discover many interesting things about ourselves when we get honest enough to stop pretending. This voyage of discovery can be the most exhilarating and rewarding one we ever undertake.

Traveling alone can be a wonderful experience and as happens on most journeys, it's almost certain you will meet interesting people on the way. One of them could be a special person in your life, but you won't know unless you decide to start on the road. Travel well!

BIBLIOGRAPHY

This is in no way intended to be a definitive reading list. However, since there is not a large body of literature addressed to men, I think it is worth noting these books which I have personally found interesting and generally helpful in coming to terms with relationship problems.

BECOMING SINGLE, *How to survive when a relationship ends*, Hamish Keith and Dinah Bradley, Sydney, Simon & Schuster, 1991.

BEFORE YOU LOVE AGAIN, *Starting a successful new relationship*, John Hosie, Sydney, Millennium Books, 1993.

EARTH HONOURING, *The new male sexuality*, Robert Lawler, Sydney, Millennium Books, 1990.

IRON JOHN, *A book about men*, Robert Bly, Reading, MA, Addison-Wesley, 1990.

MANHOOD, *A book about setting men free*, Steve Biddulph, Sydney, Finch Publishing, 1994.

THE ART OF LIVING SINGLE, *Your complete guide to enjoying life on your own*, Dr Michael S. Broder, Melbourne, Information Australia, 1994.